WWW~ Shadow of the Chameleon

A Novel by

Stuart Nelsen Speer

John & Julia Munson
3206 Ridge Street
Calumet, MI   49913

Copyright 1998 Stuart Speer
Cover Design © 1998 Press-TIGE Publishing

All rights reserved, including the right to reproduce this book
or portions therein in any form whatsoever.

For information address:
Press-Tige Publishing
291 Main Street
Catskill, NY 12414

First Press-Tige Edition 1998

Printed in the United States of America

ISBN# 1-57532-042-8

For Judy

CHAPTER ONE
THE PHANTOM VOICE

"...*no hope---no hope---no hope...*"

Mr. Ivanov and I were alone in his dingy print shop. Neither of us had said a word.

"...*no hope---no hope---no hope...*"

The noise from the shop's machines almost drowned the strange voice out, but I could hear it, and I had the creepy feeling I'd heard it before.

One of the presses finished its job, gave out a final whine, and shut down. Now I could hear and now I was sure. It was the cold dead voice from the worst nightmare I'd ever had.

A thousand tiny ants scurried up my neck and I'd have run from the shop if Mr. Ivanov hadn't been blocking the way.

He stood in front of me muttering in Russian. Then he said, "I am hearing this from a week. Is Ivanov crazy?"

I swallowed hard. "Huh-uh, it's real."

"If is real, is hiding."

He looked as scared as I felt, scared enough to bolt. But he lived there, he had no place else to go.

Not me. I can—

What? Run like a chicken?

No, truth was, I was even more afraid of looking like a coward than I was of the nightmare voice.

Mr. Ivanov picked up a box of paper and started loading it into the press that had stopped. He kept checking the dark corners of the shop like he thought a tiger might leap out. I could see he was way too freaked to help. I'd have to find the voice alone. Find it, and shut it up.

I took a deep breath, swallowed hard, and went once around the front of the shop, my hand cupped to my ear. I decided the voice wasn't coming from the front, so I stood on a box of printing paper and took a quick look around the back.

Yech!

Mr. Ivanov was a good friend and a great printer, but even

my room was neater than this. The floor was covered with dirty torn scraps of paper and dozens of empty boxes. There was no telling what sort of nastiness was back there, but I had the sinking feeling I was going to find out.

Two humongous presses blocked my way, and, as I slipped between them, my stupid shoe got hung up on their legs. I bent over to get it loose, but the smell of printing chemical made my eyes and nose sting, and I had to stand back up.

"...*no hope---no hope---no hope...*"

Now it was making fun of me.

I tugged on my trapped leg, and a gigantic rat ran out from under one of the machines. I jerked my foot loose, hopped on a wobbly table, and pulled my knees up to my chest.

Bogus!

I mean, I'd only wanted to pick up my posters, but there I was again in the middle of someone else's mess.

One of the table legs groaned and shifted underneath me. I stuck out a hand and steadied myself against the greasy side of a printing machine.

Forget this.

"Wherever it's coming from," I said, "it's not back here."

"Is not anywhere, is everywhere. Is ghost. Ivanov must be going back to Russia where we are not having ghosts."

"There aren't any ghosts in Chicago, Mr. Ivanov."

"You sure?"

"Sure, I'm sure," but I wasn't.

I sat on the table and pretended to check out the rear of the shop. After a few seconds, I hopped off and slipped back to the front. As soon as I reached the counter the voice shut up.

"Listen, Mr. Ivanov, do you, like, have any enemies?"

"No enemy. Working all days. Not having time for enemy."

"Maybe it's a joke."

"Is 'no hope' American joke?"

"No, not really."

He rubbed an ink-stained hand on the gray stubble of his chin.

"You are good detective, you are helping Ivanov. You are helping, I am selling you posters; half price."

I picked up one of the posters. The life-size face of a boy smiled back from the glossy paper. Intelligent brown eyes, curly brown hair, sparkling white teeth. Mr. Ivanov had made him look so smooth I could hardly believe he was me.

Across the top the poster read, "WWW DETECTIVE AGENCY," and beneath my picture, "Lost things found. Mysteries explained. Not expensive. I am thirteen. I have references. Signed, William Wordsworth Williamson, Detective. Call 312/ 555-1393 before 10:00 on school nights, and before midnight on weekends.

More than anything else, I wanted that poster to be true. I wanted to be a detective like my dad had been. Trouble was, I was acting more like some feeble twit. Here was the case I'd always dreamed of, and I'd been scared off by a rat.

Wasn't even that big, maybe just a fat mouse.

"I'll help you, Mr. Ivanov, but you don't have to give me the posters for half price."

"In America all peoples are getting paid. Is working in America. I am paying, you paying, nothing free, okay?"

"Okay."

I took some wadded ones out of my pocket and counted out ten bucks. Mr. Ivanov gathered the money and went to the other end of the counter to put it in his cash drawer. He turned as if he were going to say something, but before he could speak, the front door opened and a woman came in. He would have to forget about the ghost for a while, and tend to this live customer.

I pulled a stool from under the counter and climbed on. From my new perch I could see the whole back of the shop. It was straight out of a horror movie. I'd told Mr. Ivanov the voice wasn't coming from there, but...

"*No hope---no hope---no hope...*"

It's back there for sure.

Mr. Ivanov gave me a look like a sick puppy. There was no doubt about it. Nightmare or no nightmare, I'd have to find out who or what was hiding in the back, in the dark.

The weird voice no-hoped about six times, then stopped. Mr. Ivanov went back to writing his order.

That's an idea. Write it all down.

The counter top was covered with scraps from printing jobs. I flipped a pink page over to its blank side. I'd put it all on paper, flush the lame ghost crap and look at the facts.

1. **NO SUCH THING AS GHOSTS**
2. Not a joke
3. No enemies
4. Voice is coming from somewhere in the shop
5. Says "no hope", or "know-a-hope", maybe,

"New Hope."

I tried to force my brain to do what my favorite author, Professor Terry R. Denison suggested in his book, Denison on Detection. I tried to switch from the creative right side to the rational left.

DETECTIVE'S CREDO: Mental control, factual observation, reasoned deduction, decisive action. - DENISON

I looked around the shop as calmly as I could. The Professor had said the scene of the crime must be "...experienced, and understood". What was it about this place? What was it that made this place?

Machines. The place is full of machines.

I'd just written "Machines" on my list and underlined it when Mr. Ivanov returned from his customer.

"In Russia, we were having always secret police microphones. Is same in Chicago?"

"No, can't do that kind of thing here, it's not legal. Besides, microphones listen, this thing talks. Must be some kind of machine, though. There's not enough room in here for someone to hide."

"Is sad machine saying, 'no hope'. Maybe is having ghost."

"No, Mr. Ivanov, no machine ghosts, no ghosts. Period."

Got to convince him and me.

I checked my notes again. "With all the noise around here, I can't be positive it is saying 'no hope.' It sounds like 'hope,' but it might be 'New Hope'."

"What is meaning 'new hope?'"

New Hope was my hope. It was where I went for therapy to strengthen my leg and straighten my foot. It was the place that could free me from my hideous orthopaedic shoe.

But to anybody else...

"Never mind. Maybe it's 'Hope' like a girl's name. You know, like Hope what's-her-name, the tv weather lady."

His eyes brightened. "Bob Hope is some famous."

Dad's comedian?

"Where'd you hear about him?"

"Ivanov is *citizen*. Is also man named Hope from fixing copy machines. No, is maybe, Dope."

"Nobody's named Dope, Mr. Ivanov, got to be Hope."

Put Dope on the test, and they'd have deported you.

"This Hope guy," I said, "the one from fixing the copy

machine, you remember his first name?"

"Is on bill." he pulled open a file drawer, and searched through the mess inside. "Here. Copyco is company. Man is Hope, first name N-O-A-H. How you are saying?"

"It's pronounced no-uh. Was he here last week?"

"Da, last week."

When the voice started.

"Which machine did he fix?"

He came around the counter and led the way to the back of the shop.

"Is machine, Hope is fix timing." He bent over and opened a side panel. Inside the machine was a bunch of gears, pulleys, and belts. They were all grungy black, so the skinny tan box in the middle of them stood out like a Twinkie in a mud puddle.

I reached in, pulled it out, and read the label on the front. "Looks like a telephone pager. Check it out."

Mr. Ivanov took the box in his big hand, turned it around, and read. "'Copyco, Chicago, Illi-noise,' what is for?"

"I think it's Noah Hope's pager. My dad used to have one like it. His office would buzz him, and he'd call in. This one must have some kind of speaker deal instead of a buzzer, though. That is, if it's what's doing the talking."

Mr. Ivanov gave me a kindly look. "Is not talking. Machine is not talking."

I could almost hear Professor Denison's voice...

Practical demonstration is the most powerful persuader. -DENISON

"Come outside, Mr. Ivanov. Maybe I—maybe we can make it talk."

Mr. Ivanov didn't have a phone. He always said the shop was too noisy for one. We went outside to the corner pay phone. I put in a quarter and called the number on the Copyco sticker.

A woman answered. "Thank you for choosing Copyco. How may I direct your call?"

"Would you please have Mr. Noah Hope paged and ask him to call WW Williamson at 555-1393?"

"555-1393, I'll have Mr. Hope call, sir. Thank you for choosing Copyco."

I hung up. "That's my home number, but I just want him paged. If he calls at home, maybe I'll have him check about fixing the school's copy machine. It's stuck on two copies."

Mr. Ivanov grumbled something in Russian. "We are not

hearing your phone on my sidewalk. Ivanov must be in shop for customer."

"No, Mr. Ivanov, you don't understand. We're not waiting for my phone, we're waiting for the pager to—Oh well, you'll see."

When we got back to the shop, it was dead silent. I'd been in the place hundreds of times. This was the first time the nasty black machines hadn't been clattering and clanking and trying to get at me. They were even creepier this way.

Stay cool, just stay cool.

I sat down at the counter. Mr. Ivanov sat beside me, shaking the little plastic box, looking at it suspiciously.

"Is no good." He held the pager to his ear.

"Noah Hope---Noah Hope---Noah Hope..."

He gave a shout and flung it across the room.

"Easy, Mr. Ivanov." I went over, picked it up, flipped a switch on its side, and handed it back.

"Noah Hope must have left this in your copy machine. Now, every time they page him, your ghost says No-ah Hope. I'll bet Mr. Hope will be glad to get this back, though he must have another one, or they wouldn't still be paging him."

Mr. Ivanov stared at me. "Neuzheli, Malchek! You are *most* detective. Ivanov can say this, you have a real amazement."

I left the print shop feeling fine. I'd found the "ghost" and shut it up. I'd saved ten dollars on the posters, and even minus the quarter I'd blown on the phone, I still had nine dollars and seventy-five cents left.

I walked past my old school, Parker Elementary. Somehow, it looked smaller, but then I wasn't a little kid any more. I'd had my first real case, and I'd solved it, no sweat. I felt up, really up, like I could do anything, so I was kind of glad when I saw some poor little kid lying scrunched up on the sidewalk. I hurried up to see if a professional detective could help.

I bent down beside him. It was Chris Hebert, *my best friend*. "Chris! What's the matter? What happened?"

He was rolling around moaning. "Gangies. Punched me in the guts."

I helped him to his feet. "Did they rob you?"

He was still doubled up. "No, they wanted me to tell, but I wouldn't so they just hit me."

"Tell? Tell what?"

"Tell them where you were. They didn't want me, they were after you."

CHAPTER TWO
THE BLACK PANTHER

Some gangie creeps had beaten up my best friend, but only because they couldn't find me. My knees felt like rubber and my hands were shaking; partly because I was scared, but mostly because I was mad.

I steadied Chris by his shoulders. "Who was it, the Vipers?"

He straightened and groaned. "Yeah, four of them."

I took a quick look up and down the street.

"Don't worry," he said, "they're gone."

But they always came back, and it was way bad news when they did. They smashed what they didn't steal and stomped anyone who got in their way.

One time they caught me on the old bridge and threw my books in the river. Then they grabbed me and held me upside down over the railing. They would've dropped me, too, but this guy saw us and made them put me down. Another time they stole my Bulls jacket, and once they hit me with my clipboard and made my ear bleed. They'd done lots of other chicken stuff, too, but before I'd been just one of the kids they picked on. This time I was the one they wanted.

"Come on, Chris, let's get home. They might come back."

Home was the Park Manor apartments about a mile across town. Chris lived a couple of floors below me with his mother and father, but my mom and I had lived alone since my dad died, a year and a half ago next month.

When I'd been at Parker Elementary, Chris and I used to walk home from school together, but this year I'd started seventh grade at Morrison Middle School and Chris was still in fifth at Parker. Since Morrison was just across the park from home, I wouldn't even have been around to help him if I hadn't had to pick up my posters at Mr. Ivanov's.

Chris still looked pretty scared, and was holding his stomach again. I glanced behind us. There was a police car caught in traffic about half a block back. Nobody would bother us at least while he was around.

I decided to try to get Chris's mind off his stomach and the

Vipers. "I'm glad it's fall. I like the way the street trees all go yellow. Dad used to say they looked like soldiers standing in a row. He'd go up and inspect them, just like a real army."

Chris pumped quietly along beside me. He took his hand off his stomach and reached into his pocket. "I almost forgot, I have a trasher, but it's from the school trash."

Only a few people know what a trasher is. I'd thought them up a couple of years before when Chris had been grounded off tv for doing experiments with his mother's perfume. He'd always been a tv freak, and without something else to do he'd have gone totally nuts. Actually, I didn't completely think trashers up. I kind of got them from <u>Denison on Detection</u>. It had a whole chapter just on trash. Trash from the wastebasket, vacuum, outdoor trash can, you name it. Professor Denison said criminals always try to get rid of evidence, and that the trash was the first place to look. That was kind of like the trasher game. I'd get something out of the building trash, and have Chris try to figure out which of the tenants had thrown it away.

The first time we played I had to talk him into it, but now he always wanted to play, and it was getting kind of old.

Still, if it'll get his mind off those creeps...

I held out my hand and he slapped a grungy red pencil into my palm.

I rolled it between my fingers and checked it out. "Well, the eraser's been chewed off and about half the paint's been nibbled so it probably isn't a teacher's." I pressed it to my nose. "Smells like kid slobber."

"What kid?"

I took another look at what was left of some advertising on the side of it. "Looks like one of your dad's pencils, but you don't chew. I'd guess you gave it to one of the kids in your class, and they gnawed it."

He jumped around like he had to go to the bathroom. "What kid?"

Good old trashers.

"That Goober—what's his name—Johnson, the kid who eats anything."

"Awesome, dude, but he didn't eat the wood."

"Well, almost anything." I handed the half-eaten pencil back.

"Andrea Braintree guessed, too," he said, "but it took her two tries."

Andrea—

Andrea I'd tried to forget. But it isn't easy to forget two black eyes, a bloody nose, and a loose tooth.

"Is she still karate kicking people?"

Chris stuck the pencil in his pocket. "She's a brown belt now and—Oh, you mean *that*. Hey, she told me she was sorry about that. Besides, it was kind of your fault."

"Was not."

"But it was your board, and you kicked it first. You just shouldn't have held it in front of your face for her turn."

"Well, of course it broke when she kicked it, I cracked it."

He smiled. "Sure, I know. Anyway she couldn't get the other trasher so at least she isn't as smart as you."

"What other trasher?"

But he ducked into a grocery store we were passing. I did a quick check of the street for Vipers, and went in after him. He was right where I'd thought he'd be, the candy aisle.

"What other trasher?"

He looked up from the candy. "I thought you could get even with her if we had a trasher contest. But this one was way too hard for her. You probably couldn't get it either."

He turned back to the candy, checking me out of the corner of his eye. "Wish I had some money, I'd get a peanut butter cup."

I was going to buy the little sneak something with my "no hope" money, anyway. "You tell me about the other trasher, and I'll buy you some peanut butter cups."

"Deal."

He reached for one of the bright orange package of Reese's peanut butter cups, but a thick hairy arm came from behind and snatched the whole box off the shelf. I turned to see who the creep was and found myself staring at an ugly green snake on a black T-shirt. Inside the shirt was Chockie Bortka, chief creep of the Vipers. The guy who'd held me over the bridge.

He stuffed the candy box under his arm. "I been looking for you, Boot. I see you're buyin' for the midget. What you gettin' me?"

"That's okay," Chris said, "you can have mine."

Chockie reached across my face to the candy shelf; the black panther tatoo on his forearm writhing and snarling with every move.

"I'm hungry today," he said and pulled a box of Bit-O-Honey off the shelf. "Hope your pig old-man has a charge account here. Oh, now I forgot, the jerk got hisself killed, didn't he."

I took a swing at him with my roll of posters, but he grabbed my wrist and twisted the posters out of my hand.

"What's this your hittin' poor old Chockie with, Boot?" He spread the roll open. "Aw, come on, you gotta be kiddin'. You a detective? I gotta tell you, Boot, the pigs don't want no cripples."

"Who you calling 'pigs,' Bortka?" The voice came from behind him. Chockie swung around to pound whoever it belonged to. But when he saw it belonged to a big cop his jaw dropped and so did my posters.

Get o-u-t-t-a here.

I grabbed Chris and the posters and beat it for the street.

"He knows where we live," I said, "He'll come after us as soon as that cop's through with him."

I stepped off the curb waving my hand over my head. A dirty gray cab pulled up.

"I don't have any money," Chris said.

"This'll be your candy bar."

We jumped in and I gave the driver our address. He fiddled with his paperwork for what seemed like forever, called in on his radio, then slowly pulled away from the curb. I craned my neck around to check the grocery.

No sign of him.

"That dip," Chris said, "he's the one who had them beat me up. My dad says the cops should bust all those Vipers' heads."

I flashed on the big cop pounding Chockie into the ground, but I knew it wouldn't happen. My dad had been a detective lieutenant on the drug squad. He dealt with scum everyday, but he never beat someone up for being an ugly creep.

The cabby slammed on his brakes to miss something in the street. We had to grab the raggedy seat covers to keep from falling on the floor. I'd been desperate to get away from the grocery and I'd stopped a pretty crummy cab. It smelled like a gym sock and Chris's skate board would've gotten over potholes better.

Cruddiest cab in Chicago—and slowest.

But we finally struggled home and I hopped out and stood on the sidewalk waiting for the bad news.

"Four-fifty," the driver said.

I got five of my dollar bills out and handed them over. It was a lousy deal, but better than being stomped by Chockie.

The driver poked his hand back with my change pinched in his fingers. Fifty cents, enough for a soda. I told him he could keep it. He muttered something, gunned the engine, and chugged off in a cloud of blue smoke.

Like, you're welcome.

We went up through the courtyard in front of our apartments, and as we got near the front door I saw a tough looking dude sitting in the middle of the front steps. He had on a black T-shirt, but I couldn't see if it had a snake on it or not.

"Chris, is that one of the guys who beat you up?"

"Might be the guy who was in the car. Is that a Viper shirt?"

"Can't tell, but he's sure ugly enough."

Chris was a little ahead of me. He squeezed past the dude, and I followed. We had just gotten to the front door when he stood up. It was a Viper shirt.

"Missed you at school, Boot."

I shoved Chris through the door.

"Call the cops!"

He stumbled into the lobby then sprinted for the elevators. The Viper creep grabbed at me, but I swung through the big glass door, pushed it shut, and wedged my body against it. I glanced over my shoulder. None of the other elevators were open.

Stupid things, come on, come on!

The shoving on the door eased. I looked around just as the Viper lunged at the glass. I jumped back, he flew through the door, and sprawled onto the Lobby floor.

I ran for the stairway, jerked open the door, and got up the first, and was on the second flight when I heard the stairway door bang. Footsteps were coming two steps at a time.

Gotta lose him!

I reached the second floor door, yanked it open, and slammed it without going through then I climbed to the landing above, and crouched.

Don't breathe...

And it worked! The punk went to the second floor, and I ran on up the stairs. Just as I opened the fifth floor door, I heard a downstairs door bang. Footsteps started up again. Faster.

I stumbled down the hall. My leg wobbled, gave out. I dropped to all fours, crawled the last few feet to my door, and reached the key to the lock.

Here he comes!

I twisted the key, rolled through the door, and slammed it on his arm. He screamed and collapsed in the hall. The door swung lazily back open. I put my foot against it, slammed it again, and the heavy lock clicked.

I got up and hobbled to the phone to call the cops. The red message light was flashing on the answering machine.

Did Chris call? Is he okay?

I punched the play button, and heard the cold hateful voice of Chockie Bortka.

"You're *dead meat*, Boot. You <u>and</u> the midget."

CHAPTER THREE
GHOST WRITING

There always seems to be at least one siren screaming in the neighborhood, but these were really loud, really close. I got to the window just as three police cruisers screeched to a halt in front of the apartments. Two cops leaped from each car and ran toward the building.

I stumbled back to the front of the apartment and spoke through the door. "Listen, man, about twenty cops just pulled up, and they all have shotguns."

The creep kicked at the door. "You'll be sorry for this, punk. Don't nobody screw with the Vipers. <u>Nobody</u>."

But he didn't hang around. I watched through the peep hole as he ran down the hall and out of sight. Once I was sure he was gone, I struggled over to the couch and collapsed. My foot was throbbing, my hands were shaking, but I'd outsmarted a gangie and I felt good.

"Bam! Bam! Bam!" A night-stick on the front door.

"Police, open up!"

I hobbled over, peeked, and opened the door to a pair of uniformed cops.

"You Williamson?" the Sergeant asked.

"Yes, sir."

"We had a report of a homicide at this address."

"Not homicide, Sergeant. My friend Chris must have gotten a little—Chris! Gotta see if he's alright!"

"He's alright. He's alright," the Sergeant said. "Your buddy's okay. We have a team at his place. But just what <u>is</u> the trouble here?"

"It was this guy...

Precise physical description is critical to fugitive apprehension. -DENISON

"White male, five foot ten, skinny, had a scraggly moustache, Viper gang shirt. Tried to beat—assault us. Went down the stairs."

The Sergeant motioned to his partner, and she ran for the stairway door. He pulled his walkie-talkie off of his shoulder.

"All units, suspect is a white male, five-ten, thin build, scraggly moustache, wearing Viper gang colors. Negative code zero zero—repeat, negative zero zero, probable simple assault. Last seen on east stairwell."

The Sergeant and I stood in the apartment doorway. He was listening to his walkie-talkie. I was worrying about Chris.

He gets so scared.

The Sergeant turned his walkie-talkie down and clipped it back on his shoulder. "Got a few questions for my report. Mind if I come in?"

I led the way to the sofa.

"I'll need your full name for the report."

"William Wordsworth Williamson, the third."

His head bobbed back. "<u>Wordsworth</u>? You aren't Woody Williamson's boy, are you?"

"Yes sir."

"No kidding? Well, yeah, I should a known. You got his good looks. Bet the girls follow you like cats. Listen, I sure was sorry about what happened to your dad. He was a good cop, good friend, too. Anyway, Bill, or are you a Woody, too?"

"William, or WW."

"Okay, uh, William, what's the problem here?"

I told him about Chockie and the other Viper creep. He listened and wrote on a form he had fastened to an aluminum clip board.

"So you was never actually hit."

"They hit my friend, but not me. Thing is, I think the Vipers—that Chockie'll try again. He looked real mad at the store."

"Yeah, I'm not surprised that he—" His walkie-talkie squawked and he unclipped it. "Say again," A garbled voice came over the speaker. "Looks like the suspect was driving a stolen car. Can't find him though."

He pulled a carbon copy of his report off and handed it to me. "Have your mom give us a call if she has any questions."

"Sure, okay."

But I knew I wouldn't tell her about any of this. She didn't like cops, hated them, really. She blamed them for Dad's death.

The Chief, himself, had been at Dad's funeral. He gave the eulogy. He said Dad had been the finest officer he had ever had the privilege of knowing. But Mom wouldn't talk to him or any of the other cops. And she hadn't since.

"Don't worry too much about them Vipers," the Sergeant said "I'll tell the guys to put a little extra heat on them. We'll keep their scabby heads down until this blows over. Listen, I gotta get back on patrol. Anything else I can do?"

"No, but I'd better go check on Chris."

We rode down in the elevator together. I got off at Chris's floor and rang his bell. As soon as he answered I could see he was okay.

"Wow!" he said, "did you see all those cops?"

"I saw. Nice work."

"I said there was a murder so they'd come quicker. I hope they bashed that guy's head in."

"He got away. And forget about head bashing."

I reached into my pocket and felt my shrunken wad of bills. I'd blown five bucks on a cab ride and twenty-five cents on a phone call, but I was still four seventy-five to the good and I had an urge to spend some dough on something fun.

"Your rents home?"

"No, and Mom won't be home for," he looked at his watch, "for at least a half an hour. Wait till she hears about this."

"Let's keep this a secret. Otherwise my mom'll hear about it and you know how she is."

"Well, okay," Chris said, "but somebody'll probably tell her anyway. All those cops and everything."

"Can't help that, but let's keep it quiet."

"If I've gotta."

Looks so disappointed.

"Hey, you want to go to Pumperdingle's and get some ice cream or something?"

"No way," he said, "Chockie might be out there."

"I doubt it. The cops would've grabbed anyone in a Viper shirt. Besides, it's just down the street."

"But..."

I picked his baseball cap up and tossed it to him. "It'll be okay. We'll just be gone for a minute."

"Okay," he said, "but I'd better leave a note for Mom."

As soon as we reached the sidewalk, I was sorry I'd thought of Pumperdingle's. My heavy orthopedic shoe was chaffing my ankle and my leg was throbbing big-time from running up the stairs and Pumperdingle's looked like it'd moved further down the block. I tried not to hobble, bit my lip, and kept my mind busy by listening to Chris yak about school.

We made it to Pumperdingle's without any Vipers and stopped inside the front door to scope out the most excellent desserts rotating in their glass display-case. There were bright yellow pieces of lemon meringue pie and tall chunks of black forest cake with maraschino cherries peaking out from between the layers. We watched as a bright green piece of lime pie floated by followed by cheesecake with blueberries, cheesecake with cherries, and cheesecake with strawberries.

These all looked choice, but the smell of fresh hot cinnamon told me the baker had just finished a batch of his infinitely awesome apple strudel. I forgot about my foot, about Chockie, about ice cream, pie, and cheesecake.

"Want to split a strudel?"

"A whole one?"

"Why not?"

Pumperdingle's gives you, like, gigantic servings so a whole apple strudel is majorly large. We sat in a booth and pigged. The apple goo was still warm. Chris chewed on his chunk and hummed. I checked around the room to see if any of my other friends were there.

The deli was kind of the center of the neighborhood. If you sat there for very long you'd see practically everyone. I spotted a few familiar faces including some old customers. Mr. Spotney was sitting by the front window. I'd found his keys for him after they'd been missing for a whole week. Mrs. Meyerhoff was at the carry-out counter. I'd found her high school yearbook in the Salvation Army Store's book bin while my mom and I were shopping. I figured she'd given it away by accident and I was right.

But both these cases were from before. From when I was paid in chocolate chip cookies or pats on the head. Now I was a professional. I was ready to advertise, ready to handle some real cases, paying cases.

"I should've brought my posters."

"What posters?" Chris said.

"The ones I was carrying home today." Earth to Chris. "The advertisements for my detective agency. You know, the ones Chockie tried to steal."

"Oh, yeah. Do I get one?"

"If you promise not to let my mom see it."

"Okay. That reminds me," He smiled, reached into his

pocket and pulled out a crumpled paper bag. "I have the other trasher. I picked this one special for the contest with Andrea."

I shook my head. "No way I'm doing a contest with her."

"Thing is," he said, "I already bet you could beat her."

"Oh yeah? What are the stakes?"

"Can't you think of anything but food?"

"Stakes," I said, "are the things that the winner of a bet wins. You're thinking of moo-cow steaks. What'd you bet Braintree?"

"Your fingerprint set."

I was leaning on the table with a cheek propped on one hand. I had eaten as much strudel as I could and had heard as much from Chris as I needed. I was thinking.

Would they convict a thirteen-year-old of murder?

"Tell me, Chris. Tell me you did not bet my brand new, unopened, official, FBI fingerprint set my uncle just gave me for my birthday."

He gave me his innocent smile. "It's not like she'll win or anything. You can beat her e-easy. Besides, it was the only thing I could think of that she might want."

"I'll just have to tell her the bet's off."

"Don't you want to know what kind of stakes she had?"

"It wouldn't make any difference."

"Not even a computer?"

A computer. The one major piece of detective equipment I didn't have.

"But her dad gave her that computer," I said. "He'd foam if she lost it."

"She said it didn't matter. She said you'd chicken out anyway."

"Chicken? She said I'd—"

"Chicken."

The waitress came up. "You boys want anything else?"

"Yeah, uh, yes, ma'am. Could we have the rest to go?"

"I'll getcha a couple of bags."

While we waited for the bags, Chris tried to drive me nuts by tapping his knife handle on the table top.

"Well," he said, "do you want to see it or not?"

"I'm not saying I'll do it, but since you went to all this trouble, I'll take a look at your clues."

He wiggled happily, smoothed his crumpled bag out on the table, reached in, and got out a fistful of paper bits.

"This is a *real* one. Right out of our building's trash. Alls you gotta do is figure out who threw it away."

I put my finger on a piece of the trash, dragged it across the table, and picked it up. At least it didn't smell as bad as some of the other trashers he'd come up with.

"Looks like a claim check from the Insta-Clean cleaners down the block." I picked up the other scraps of paper and snuck a glance at Chris. He was grinning.

Evil child-genius.

"A candy wrapper; Toblerone Chocolate Candies, Switzerland. One empty matchbook from The Central Bank of Chicago. One—What's this?"

"That's the best one, but I can't help you. That wouldn't be fair to Andrea."

Fair?

Like she'd been fair to me—to us. I mean she always got first choice. We always let her have her way, but, no, that wasn't good enough. She had to be with her stuck-up rich friends. Well, that was fine with me.

But why make Chris suffer? It doesn't cost anything to look.

I spread the puzzling last clue out on the table top. It was a brown strip of paper with $2,000 printed on it in orange ink. I could see the two ends had been pasted together to make a loop.

Interesting.

"This *is* a good one, Chris. You're really catching on."

"Then you'll do it?"

"Let me take this thing home. I want to look at it in better light."

The waitress came back with our bags. We shoved our leftover strudel into them and went to the front to pay. I leaned close to the window and checked the sidewalk.

No Chockie. No Vipers.

Chris pressed his nose against the glass. "Looking for Chockie?"

"Naw, just looking."

On the way back the apartments my leg got to feeling a little better. Must have been the strudel. I wasn't even that worried about Chockie. The police were looking for him, harder than usual, and his creepy friend would tell him about getting chased away from our apartments.

This is my block. These are my friends. He wouldn't dare pick on me here again.

But he had dared. The glass door to Park Manor had been spray painted with bright green gang signs and a message.

"Skweeler Pig Dies!!!"

Chris's pressed against my side. His eyes filled with tears. "They're gonna kill us, aren't they?"

I wrapped my arm around him. "They just talk tough. They don't kill people. They just want to scare us. Don't worry, the apartment manager will call the police and they'll catch these morons, I promise."

Chris wiped his eyes on his jacket sleeve. "Don't let them kill me, WW."

"Don't be silly. Nobody's going to kill anybody. Anyway it's me they want, and I'm not going to let them get me or you, okay? Now let's get home before everyone wonders where we are."

I went with Chris to his door then took the elevator on up to my apartment. Mom had dinner waiting, but my appetite had been destroyed by Chockie's threats and a couple of pounds of strudel. I sat at the table and stared at her dumb tv quiz-show.

Mom hadn't watched much tv before Dad died, never at dinner, but now she never seemed to turn it off and I was sick of it. I poked at my peas with my fork and after a few minutes asked to be excused and went to my room.

I put Chris's bag of trasher clues on my desk next to some detective stuff my Dad had given me. I had a binocular microscope, German magnifying glass, a centrifuge, and dozens of other pieces of real police equipment. It seemed a little silly using Dad's high-tech stuff to work on a trasher, but he'd always liked trashers, too. In fact he was the one who'd thought up the name.

"It's a kind of mix of 'treasure' and 'trash', and that makes sense because trash often has treasure for a sharp detective." Dad had read Professor Denison, too.

I picked up his picture from the corner of my desk. He looked so confident in his dress blue uniform. Invincible. I could almost hear the rap of his old night stick on my bedroom door as he rousted me in the morning.

If he'd been there today...

But he wasn't, and he never would be again.

I put his picture down and stared blankly at the trasher junk. The phone in the living room rang. I snapped out of it and tried to take a serious look at the clues.

It seemed pretty obvious what I needed to do to solve

WWW: Shadow of the Chameleon

Chris's puzzle:
    Cleaners' claim check: Check at the cleaners.
    Imported candy: Find out where this stuff is sold.
    Empty match book from local bank: Smoker?
    It was the band of paper that was tough. I spread it out again and pulled the two ends together with the orange printing on the outside. In big numbers it read "$2,000" and above and below that in slightly smaller type was "One Hundred Dollar Bills."

    I'd seen something like this on tv. When the kidnappers had a suitcase full of money it was always wrapped in strips of paper. This had to be one of those.

    When I overlapped the two ends of the money band to make a loop, I could see that someone had handwritten "2m, H.O." across the place where the ends met. Below that in different handwriting were the letters "C.L." and those letters were rubber-stamped over by a light blue "W" with a circle around it. I held the money band up to my magnifying glass and could see that the circle around the "W" stamp was actually tiny writing, but I couldn't make out what it said.

    Need Dad's light box.

    The light box was really just this plastic thing with several types of light bulbs inside and a clear glass top. The idea was to put evidence on the glass and use the different lights to do a close examination. I went to my closet and pulled the portable tv sized machine off the shelf.

    I spread the money band on the glass and switched on the high intensity light. It didn't help. I tried the black light which gave off very little light, but which made some kinds of inks glow. The "W" stamp did glow, but I still couldn't make out the writing. I switched off the room light and that did the trick. With the help of my magnifying glass I could see that the circle around the "W" was formed by repeating "Wraith" four times, end to end.

    Name? Word?

    I got out the dictionary.

    "Wraith \r th\ n. 1: phantom, spirit, phantasm, or ghost."

CHAPTER FOUR
THE CONTEST

It was Saturday morning. I was soaking in the tub, thinking about the two ghosts I'd met on Friday. First there was Mr. Ivanov's phony ghost and now this wraith from the trash.

"Coincidence." Hearing it out loud made it more believable so I said it again. "All just a coincidence."

The bathroom was full of steam. The mirror was fogged, and the pink tile walls were beaded with water. I watched as a two drops broke loose and raced each other down to the tub. Good old Saturday. I could relax and take as long a soak as I needed, and I needed a long one. Running from Chockie had made my leg—

Chockie—

My stomach knotted, and the once comfortable bath water turned clammy. I dragged myself up, drained, dried, dressed, and went down the hall to the kitchen.

The sun was shinning through the red-checked curtains. I pulled them back. The same tall buildings were standing where they always were.

Calm down, dude. You're safe up here.

I was alone in the kitchen, in the apartment, too. By now Mom would be at some suburban art fair trying to sell her paintings. She had a real job as a para-legal, but on weekends she sold her watercolors to make extra money.

She'd made me go with her to the malls before, but this week I'd insisted I was in middle school and could take care of myself. I kind of felt like a wuss for not going along, at least to help her set up her booth, but I was totally tired of the whole mall-art deal.

I checked the fridge and found a most excellent start for a Saturday, leftover strudel. I slipped it in the wave and returned to the fridge to scrounge.

"Hunter-gatherers" was what Ms. Finch, my Social Studies teacher said early people were. That was me. I hunted through the leftovers, gathered a slice of pepperoni pizza and a whole unopened can of lemon-lime soda. It all looked real good spread out on the table.

Sweet, sour, and salty. The three major food groups.

I sat down to my feast, but before I could take a bite the phone rang. I picked up the kitchen extension.

"Williamson's."

"Hi, it's Chris. You coming down today?"

"Soon as I eat."

"Good. We can go over to the park and look at the trees or something."

Chris wants to look at trees?

"Okay, be down in a minute."

"You gonna bring my clues?"

"They're in my jacket."

"Good, see you in a minute."

Breakfast didn't go like I'd planned. The strudel burned the roof of my mouth, and the pizza must've had a hidden chunk of anchovy in it because it tasted like Italian cat food. I cleaned up my dishes and went on down to Chris's. He was waiting in the hall.

"I like this time of year," he said as we got back on the elevator. "I like jackets, and the leaves clog the sewers."

"Why do you want the sewers clogged?"

"I don't know. Just different."

Weird kid.

We went out through the front entrance. A workman was scraping the green paint off the glass.

"I didn't tell about Chockie," Chris said.

"Good, thanks."

"I wasn't crying or nothing. We aren't afraid of Chockie, are we?"

I patted him on the shoulder. "Only thing he might do is paint us green."

We laughed and went on across the street to the park. I tried not to let Chris notice I was checking for Vipers.

The weather at the park was perfect. A wind was blowing in from Lake Michigan. The air was chilly but not real cold. In a month or so some wicked storms might blow in, but today the stiff breeze felt good.

Chris darted away, heading for the playground. "Come on. We haven't played on the stuff for ages."

By the time I caught up he was smiling at me from the splintery seat of the old teeter-totter. "Think you can budge me?"

I grabbed my end, shoved down, and hopped on.

"Ye-hah!" he yelled, as he shot up to the sky.

"You're in for it now." I pushed off from a squat and dropped him squealing back to earth. Then I moved the teeter-totter back level holding myself on my strong leg. "Too rough?"

"See if you can make me jump clear off the seat."

"You asked for it."

I tucked my leg in. "Wham!" He shot back up to about a foot off his seat.

"Do it again!"

So I did it again and again until his face started to turn green.

"I think that's enough."

I eased him down, and he wobbled off and leaned against the ladder of the slipper-slide looking woozily at his watch.

"What's the matter?" I said. "Missing one of your cartoons?"

"Just wondered what time it was."

He looked across the street. His eyes widened. I turned to see what he was looking at, and there she was, waiting on the far corner for the light to change.

She was taller, almost my height. Her light-brown hair was longer and she was wearing lipstick, but I recognized Parker Elementary's own karate-kicking Andrea Braintree. She stepped off the curb when the light changed, walked quickly across the street, and right up to us.

"Hi, Chris. What're you doing here, WW?"

What do you mean...

"I'm playing in *my* park. What are you doing here?"

She straightened up. "Chris asked me to meet him here to help him with his math."

I looked at Chris.

"Okay, okay," he said. "Don't get excited. I have this plan. You'll see. It's gonna be fun like it used to."

He turned and walked back toward the center of the park acting like nothing had happened. "Isn't it a nice day? Don't you just love the—"

"What's going on?" Andrea said.

"I think Chris is trying to get us to do his game."

"You mean that trashy thing? Aren't you boys a little old for dumb games?"

"It's 'trasher,'" I said, "and it isn't dumb. Besides he said you wanted to play."

"He imagines things."

Chris looked back at her. "You used to, too."

That was true enough. Both of them had been pretty good at imagining back when Saturdays had been the three of us. But that was before she changed. Before all she wanted to do was play inside. Before she got too good for us.

She walked past Chris and gave his hair a rub. "You have to grow up sometime, homeboy. Anyway, I looked at the trashy stuff. It was way too easy for a contest."

She looked at me. "I suppose you figured out about the money band and the writing on it."

She *knows*.

I tried to look unimpressed. "Sure, I figured it out, except the rubber-stamp "W". That's the only hard part."

"There wasn't anything hard about the stupid stamp."

"Wait a minute," Chris said, "we have to have a meeting before we start."

"Start what?" I said. "I didn't say I'd do anything."

Andrea smiled real smirky. "Afraid of losing?"

"I didn't say I wouldn't. I said I didn't."

Chris hopped between us. "Remember she's betting her computer."

I glared at her. "Are you serious?"

She elbowed Chris out of the way. "Of course I'm serious, and it sure beats your crummy finger-print set."

"That happens to be a *real* finger-print set."

"My computer happens to be a *real* computer."

Chris was between us again. "That's fair. That's fair. Everything's real. That makes it fair. Right?"

Chockie's snake eyes had stared me down. Her eyes weren't mean as his, but...

"What would you want with a fingerprint set?" I said.

"What would *you* want with it? Your mom'll just throw it away like everything else."

That wasn't fair. Maybe, Mom had thrown away a lot of the detective stuff I inherited from Dad, his medals, badge, other things, too, but that was right after he died. She was upset and she'd had too much to drink.

Isn't her business anyway.

"You're the one with problems. Your Dad's gonna kill you when he finds out you lost your computer."

"You're the one who's gonna lose. You're gonna lose your stupid nose."

Chris pushed us apart. "No hitting, you guys. Come on, WW, why don't we just do the trasher. It'll be fun like it used to."

It is a computer

Chris got me by the sleeve of my jacket and pulled me over to a park bench. "I thought up some good rules. The first is, since it's my trasher, I get to be captain."

Andrea followed us to the bench. "Captain? What does a captain do?"

"You know, like the cop movies. The captain sits in this glass office and yells at people."

"Wait a minute, Chris," I said. "You mean you want us to pretend we work for you?"

"Yeah."

Andrea had circled behind the bench. "Listen, Williamson I'm not working with him. That's dumb. No bet."

"It's not dumb," Chris said. "It's real. Cops work together, but the one who figures it out gets the credit."

"The collar," I said.

His forehead wrinkled.

"What's the matter, Chris?" Andrea said, "I thought you were the expert on cop movies. The collar is the credit for the arrest."

"Only we aren't really going to arrest anybody," I said.

Andrea snorted. "You aren't much of a detective if you think that, Williamson. That money band is the kind kidnappers get their ransoms in."

Not much of a...

"Look, Braintree, I'm more of a detective than you'll ever be. I could figure this out before you even got started."

"Well then," she said, "maybe you'd like to bet."

Snotty little...

"Okay. I bet you my new fingerprint set to your dorky computer that I can figure out who threw this trasher stuff away before you can. Deal?"

"Deal. But none of that dumb captain stuff."

"No Chris, no deal."

She gave him a killer look. "I'm not going to tell him about anything I find out, if it's any good."

"You won't find anything good."

Chris got up from the bench twisting his hands. "Come on, you guys. Let's look at the clues."

I wasn't sure if Andrea was still in on the bet or not. The Chris thing might have screwed it up. But if I asked her now she might officially back out, and I knew now I wanted to beat her, beat her bad.

I pulled the clues out of my pocket and spread them on the park bench. Andrea picked up the two thousand dollar moneyband and gave me a suspicious look. "Are you sure all this stuff was in the trash container behind your apartment building?"

"That's the rule," I said.

"I still don't see anything interesting about the "W" stamp," she said. "And who wrote this 'Wraith' on here? Is this one of your dumb tricks, Williamson?"

"If you'd looked carefuller, Braintree, you'd have noticed the ring around the "W" is made out of the word 'Wraith'. I looked it up, it means 'ghost'. All I did was write it down so I wouldn't forget it."

"Ghost?" Chris said. "Ghosts and money. This is gonna be good. Maybe somebody needed two thousand dollars to get rid of a ghost."

"More likely," Andrea said, "Wraith is someone's name."

"It might be the trasher guy's name," I said. "I think I'll look for a rich ghost who's a candy freak."

"Not me." She held up the laundry claim check. "*I'm* looking for a candy eating rich ghost in a <u>clean</u> sheet."

CHAPTER FIVE
THE TRAIL OF CLUES

Andrea and I sat on the park bench listening to Chris rattle on with his list of trasher contest rules.

He was starting on number eleven when she held up her hand. "You can be the captain under one condition. <u>No more rules</u>. The only rule is the first one to figure out who threw this trasher stuff away wins."

"But I only have six more—"

Her hand went up again. "No more."

He sat down frowning and grumbling. Andrea went back to looking through the clues. I didn't want her to get ahead of me, so I started sorting through the clues, too.

Cleaners' claim check, matchbook, candy bar wrapper, and the strange money band. All had been in the building trash in a paper sack.

Unless Chris <u>has</u> been cheating.

I poked him in the ribs. "You didn't just make all this up did you?"

"Make what up?"

"The trasher, dude. You didn't just get a bunch of stuff together and pretend?"

He'd already been ticked off by Andrea, now his ears started to get red. "I did <u>not</u>. I found all those things together in the big container behind the apartments. I'd <u>never</u> make up a trasher."

"Alright, calm down." I tried to pat his hand, but he pulled it away. "Listen, I believe you, but why'd you pick this bag?"

He sniffed and rubbed his sleeve under his nose. "All the other stuff in the trash was too easy or too rotten. I kept this stuff because it had that neat money thing. Besides the bag was smoking and I thought that was, you know, a sign."

Andrea looked up from her work. "Smoking? The bag was smoking? Why didn't you say so? Was there a cigarette in it?"

"Yes—No, not in the bag, under it."

She picked up the bag and examined it. "I can't believe you had this all night, Williamson, and didn't see this."

I grabbed the bag and looked at the spot she was pointing at. There was a small burn hole in the bottom corner of the sack that was some kind of cigarette burn for sure.

I remembered the Professor's advice.

Tobacco residue is an important link to the smoker who created it. -DENISON

I rubbed the smoky stink from my nose. "It would be lots easier to find the trasher dude if we were sure he smoked."

"Wait a minute, you guys," Chris said. "You're going too fast. You gotta report what you already know."

Andrea jumped up and saluted. "Captain, sir. We know where the trasher suspect lives, sir."

I stood, twisted my hand around, and gave Chris an upside down salute. "Sir we do not know where the trasher suspect lives, sir. Detective Tomboy is only guessing."

Uh-oh.

"*Tomboy?* Who you calling a tomboy, you sexist twit? I'm no tom boy, no boy at all."

"Well ex-cuse me, but you used to—"

"What? Climb trees? Come on, get into the now, Williamson. Women climb what ever they want to. And as for the trasher, it's clear to me that a person who has cleaning done in the neighborhood and throws her or his trash in your container would live in the neighborhood. She or he probably even lives in your building."

Gets so mad so easy.

"Okay, okay," I said. "Let's just say he does live in the building. What else do we know?"

"I know I'm hungry," Chris said. "Why don't we go to my place and get some lunch?"

Andrea looked at me. "I don't care who I eat with if I'm hungry enough." She turned back to Chris. "Is it okay with your folks?"

"It was Dad's idea. He said when we got tired of the park we could come back there."

Little weasel knew all along.

"If she thinks she has to eat," I said, "I might as well come, too."

We went back to Park Manor and up to Chris's place. When we walked into his living room his dad peered out from the kitchen. "Well, well, well. What have we here? Ms. Braintree, long time no see, and WW and a mystery boy. You guys looking for free eats?"

"Can you please make us some samitches," Chris said.

"Okay." Mr. Hebert wiggled his fingers at us. "Presto-change-o, you're some sandwiches. What shall I do for my next trick?"

I was used to his dad's lame sense of humor. I'd heard the "next trick" joke about a billion times but I laughed.

"What would you like, young lady?" Mr. Hebert asked Andrea.

"Cheese, please."

"I'm sorry, we're all out of cheeseplease. Would plain cheese be okay?"

Mr. Hebert found the cheese (pimento) and made her sandwich. Then he made a pimento cheese, peanut butter, and banana sandwich for Chris.

He turned to me. "What's your poison?"

"Whatever you're having's fine."

"Brave boy. Now where did I put those bat wings?"

It wasn't bat wing, but my sandwich was strange. I did double potato chips and slipped most of the sandwich to their dog, Harold.

After lunch, we were feeling better. At least, I was. The three of us went to Chris's room and spread out the clues on his bed.

Andrea pulled a piece of paper from the evidence. "Listen, Captain Chris, sir, I want to work on my own clue."

"Okay, we can split the clues. WW, why don't you take the candy bar wrapper? You could go around and ask everybody in the building if it's theirs."

"Not everyone," I said, "just the rich people. Look at the price sticker; a dollar forty-nine."

"For that little thing?" Chris examined the candy wrapper again, shook his head, and set it back down on the bed, more carefully than he had before.

"Why don't you start with the lady in the penthouse?" I said. "If she can afford to live up there she can sure afford expensive candy."

"I didn't know there was anybody in the penthouse." Chris said.

"Yes you did. You know, the lady with the red sports car, the one you said looked spooky."

"Oh, yeah, her. I don't want to talk to her. Besides, you have to have a key to use the penthouse elevator."

"You could buzz her intercom. But never mind, it was just a suggestion."

I looked to see what Andrea was doing. "Which clue are you taking?"

She stuck something in her pocket. "Bet if I show this claim check to the people at the cleaners they can look their records and tell me whose it is."

"Wait a minute," Chris said, "that would be cheating."

"That's not cheating," I said, "that's just smart."

Wish I'd remembered to do it.

Andrea got up and headed for the door. She bumped into me on her way by.

She does smell nice. Kind of rosey.

Chris walked her to the elevator and came back tossing his apartment key from hand to hand. "Come on, I'll help you ask around about the candy."

I raised an eyebrow as high as I could. "But, Captain Chris, wouldn't <u>that</u> be cheating?"

"Captains can't cheat."

"Uh-huh. Well, the first thing I want to do is go to my place and get my posters. They won't do me any good unless I put them up. Then I'm going over to Star Market."

"But I thought we were going to ask people about the candy."

"You stay here and do that. I'll go see if anyone at the market knows who buys this Toblerone candy."

He stuck his key in his pocket. "Okay. Where is the Star Market?"

"Come on dude, the grocery store we were in yesterday. The one you've walked by about a million times."

"Oh. I didn't know it was—Are you *crazy*? You can't go there. Chockie might still be there."

But, Professor Denison understood.

The trail of clues often leads in harm's way. -DENISON

"Look, this is important to me. I know it's just a game to you, but, well, I have to follow the clues." I sounded braver than I felt. "Star Market has lots of fancy candies, closest place that does."

"Okay," he said, "but I'm going, too."

"No, you stay here. I think Chockie specially likes picking on little kids. Besides, you need to ask around about the Toblerone."

He frowned. "It isn't as important as going to the store."

"It's just as important and besides, I'll only be gone an hour or so. It'll give me a chance to put up some of my posters. I'll save one for you. We can put it up when I get back."

Chris was still grumbling when I left, but it was better to have him grumpy than to let Chockie get him again. I felt a little grouchy too. I still wasn't getting paid.

But Andrea's computer will be pay. Major big-time pay.

On my way to Star Market I went into about a dozen stores and asked if I could put up a poster. The trip took longer that way, but it also made it harder for the Vipers to spot me. By the time I got to Star Market I had only two posters left, and one of those was Chris's.

The grocery store's windows were plastered with ads for blade-cut chuck roast, canned corn, Kielbasa, Polsky Wyrobs, and other junk I'd heard of but never tried. When I got my face right next to the window I could see between the ads.

Don't see him. Don't smell him either.

I went in, staying close to a guy in a security guard's uniform. When I got to the candy aisle the peanut butter cups and the Bit-O-Honeys were back on the shelf. There was no sign of the fight with Chockie. Nothing.

Sure, like they'd put up a plaque. "On this spot, William Wordsworth Williamson *almost* got stomped."

Since it was Saturday, there was a big crowd in the store, and I kept getting bumped into by the other people checking out the fancy candies. I found some German candy bars that cost, like, three dollars, and Swiss and Dutch bars that cost even more, but no Toblerone.

I didn't want to go home with nothing and I couldn't afford the fancy candy, so I picked up a package of peanut butter cups and a Bit-O-Honey. I didn't even like Bit-O-Honey, but I picked one up anyway.

Kind of like a plaque.

I got in the checkout line. As I moved forward I read the headlines on the dopey papers that stuck out of the racks. "<u>Two Headed Baby Able To Read Own Mind!!!</u>" "<u>Is Your Child's Teacher A Space Alien?</u>"

The line inched forward and I came up beside one of those candy racks they put there to make you hungry. Right in plain sight on the top shelf was a big stack of Toblerone candy bars. I looked at the other checkout lines. They all had big piles of Toblerone. They weren't rare after all. I pulled the wrapper clue out of my pocket and sighed. Wraith had escaped.

The disappointment spoiled my appetite for candy bars, but I was already in line so I kept moving forward. Ahead of me was a large man. He wasn't Chockie Bortka, I'd looked, but I hadn't checked behind me in a while, and it was from behind that I heard the sickening crack of knuckles.

I didn't look; didn't have to. Only Chockie could crack knuckles that way. I slipped between the candy and magazine racks, shot across two lines of shoppers, threw my candy on a shelf, and ran for the back of the store.

Don't look back!

I shoved through the rear door expecting to be outside, but was in a back room full of stacks of boxes and cans. No doors, no windows. The only escape was back through the store and Chockie was out there.

Gotta hide!

I squirmed into a dark corner behind two tall stacks of boxes. When I pressed against the wall something poked me in the back. I ran my hand up behind me.

Door handle.

I squirmed around and twisted the handle. The latch released, but the door was held at the top by a slide-bolt. When I reached up to pull the bolt down I noticed a faded sign. "!!!STAY OUT-THIS MEANS YOU!!!"

Forget you, pal.

I pulled the bolt down quietly as I could, swung the door open, and looked out on trash cans, gravel—

Sky.

I slipped out and eased the door shut. I was behind the store, but I wasn't free. A ten-foot chain link fence closed off the back. I ran to the gate on the far end.

Locked!

I ran back to the other end.

Dead end!

I shook the fence in frustration and a massive heap of matted fur stirred in the corner and rose to it's feet.

CHAPTER SIX
TRAPPED

The huge dog lowered to a bristly crouch, its yellow fangs bared.

"Wham!"

The store's steel door slammed back against the building. The dog switched its head back and forth checking on who was coming but keeping me cornered.

"Shouldn't hide from me, Boot." The voice came from the other side of the row of trash cans. "If you hide, Chockie'll get mad." I could hear him prowling along the fence. "Come here you little squeal—"

He stood frozen, staring at the dog. A low growl rumbled in the dog's throat. Chockie stumbled back into the garbage cans. The dog scrambled after him and lunged at the side of his neck.

That was my chance. I ran to the back door and yanked on it.

Locked!

The dog was ripping chunks from Chockie's leather jacket. Chockie was tucked in a ball, screaming. "Help! Help! Get him off me!"

I pounded on the door. No answer. I knew I couldn't make it over the fence. I scanned the back of the building. Just above the door was a metal box like the school's burglar alarm. I traced the power cord down the door frame. If I could break the connection it might go off. I yanked on the cord as hard as I could. It popped and cracked, but didn't break.

The screaming stopped. I looked around. The dog had his jaws clamped on Chockie's throat!

I wrapped the chord around my hands, put both feet on the side of the building, and pulled so hard I came off the ground.

With a loud snap, the chord broke and I landed on my back. The alarm shrieked and the dog shrank away and cowered in the corner.

The steel door flew open. Hands grabbed me, dragged me

back into the store.

A man in a white apron was screaming in my face. "What the hell? You could of been killed! Didn't you see the sign? You stupid—could of been killed!"

Chockie was in the building too, lying motionless on the floor; bleeding from his face, hands, and neck. His jacket was shredded and he stunk of garbage.

Apron man pulled Chockie up to a chair then turned to me, calmer now. "You alright, kid?"

"Sure. Sorry about the alarm. Had to do something."

"Yeah, well at least that was smart."

Chockie was moving a little, starting to look more alive. He reached a bloody hand up to smooth his hair. That was enough of a recovery for me.

"Mister," I said, "I have to go home."

He was holding a towel to Chockie's neck and spoke over his shoulder. "You stay where you are. I'm going to get an ambulance and have you kids looked at."

I usually obey adults, especially angry ones, but I didn't want to be around when Chockie got any better. I slipped away from the crowd that had gathered and left.

My hands and especially my legs were shaking as I walked along the sidewalk. As strong as Chockie was, the dog had nearly killed him.

If it had gotten me...

A sick feeling rose up from my stomach. I ducked into an alley, threw up behind a trash can, and started shaking all over. It was like a dream; a horrible bad dream.

Why doesn't he leave me alone? I never hurt him.

I'd never felt so completely alone before. I needed to talk, to tell someone. But who? Mom?

Yeah, right, she'd freak.

And Chris was already freaked. Besides, if I told him he'd tell his rents and they'd tell Mom. Last time, when they found out somebody had stolen his hundred dollar shoes, they didn't let him out for almost two months. If they found out about this they wouldn't ever let him out.

Can't tell Andrea. She'd think I was a wimp. She'd have karateed Chockie; the dog, too.

But Chris and Andrea would already know all about this if the Vipers got to the apartments before I did. I hurried home as fast as I could and was majorly relieved to see both of them sitting on the steps, alone.

"No, Chris, you have to carry the three over to the tens place if you want it to add up right," Andrea said.

Chris looked up from the lesson. "Back already? I didn't get to ask about the candy bar, but Andrea's helping me with my homework."

Seeing Chris doing something as normal as homework made things feel more real. "Great, that's great. And don't worry about the candy bar, it wasn't much anyway."

He smiled. "Andrea's gonna show me how to do fractions, wanna help?"

"Sure." I checked the street for signs of Vipers, then sat down next to her where I could keep an eye on things.

She put her heavy math book down on the stoop. "You alright?"

"Just tired. Ran home."

She started to collect her stuff. "What makes you think the candy wasn't a good clue?"

"They sell it at Star Market, alright. But it isn't rare, they had big displays at all the checkout lines. What'd you find out at the cleaners?"

She stuffed her calculator and ruler in her book bag. "I think that's enough for now, Chris. I'll show you how to do fractions later." He was too busy admiring his completed problems to answer.

"I took the ticket into the cleaners and asked them if the clothes had been picked up," she said. "They told me the order had been picked up without a claim check, and they wanted to know if there'd been some mistake. I told them no, and left."

"Did they keep the claim check?"

"Yeah, but I have a photocopy of it. I took it at the drugstore while I was getting batteries for my calculator."

"Good work."

"Yes, I know. You don't have to tell me. What'd you do to your hand?"

My right palm had several red stripes where the alarm chord had cut and bruised. "It's nothing. But about the cleaners thing, probably our guy picked up the cleaning, but didn't have the claim check because he'd accidentally thrown it away in the trasher bag."

I tossed the empty candy wrapper to Chris. "Anyway, Captain, it seems like detective Braintree here was right. The trasher dude probably lives in the building, buys expensive candy, is careless with claim checks, maybe also careless with cigarettes. Did I miss anything?"

"As usual." Andrea had gathered all her stuff onto her lap. "You forgot that she or he is neat. She or he disposed of the candy wrapper and an empty matchbook in a paper bag. Pretty tidy, huh?"

Careless and tidy. Who's careless and tidy?

The sun had slid around to the other side of the building. The front stoop was getting chilly, and when a cool wind blew over us, we all had the same idea at once.

"Let's go inside," Chris said.

I stood up. "Yeah, we can go to my place."

We headed for the lobby. I held the door for Andrea because her arms were full of school stuff. We went to the elevators, and Chris punched the up button. The lights above the door blinked as an elevator came down. Five, four, three, two, the bell rang, the door opened, and we stepped back to let a man out. It was Mr. Katz from the fifth floor. He was in the corner of the elevator with his aluminum crutches propped out to his sides. We waited while he pushed and pulled himself out.

He moved like an old man, but, except for his stooped shoulders, he didn't look that old. He had bushy black hair, and a full beard that didn't have any gray. Sometimes I saw him in a wheelchair, but mostly he got around on crutches.

He lived right down the hall from me, so I saw him in the hallways and on the elevator all the time. I had learned he didn't say much, and that what he did say was usually pretty cold.

I grabbed the edge of the elevator door to keep it from shutting on him, but he paid no attention. He just went on past and down the hall. We got on the elevator and went up to my place.

"I feel sorry for him," Chris said, "but why's he gotta be such a crab?"

"Yeah?" Andrea said.

"How am I supposed to know?" I snapped, and they clammed up.

Mom was back from the art fair, so I went to her room to say hello. She said we could get some cookies or fruit, if we wanted. I got some cookies and led the way to my room.

I got out my light box for some show and tell. "This is what I used in order to read the tiny 'Wraiths' around the 'W' stamp."

Andrea put her hands to her cheeks. "Oh, you're so brilliant, such a genius. Where's your fingerprint set, genius?"

"I haven't opened it yet, but you can look at the box."

"Never mind, I'll own it soon enough."

I rubbed my chin and looked around the room like I was searching for something.

"Lose something?" Chris asked.

"No, just trying to figure where I'll put my new computer."

"You wish," Andrea said.

Chris handed Andrea her book bag. "No fighting, you guys. I'm the captain, remember? You have to do what I say, and I want to know what the writing on the money band means."

"Sure, Cap," Andrea said, "but Mr. know-it-all ought to be able to tell us that. What would you write on a stack of hundred dollar bills, Williamson?"

Glad I didn't tell her about the dog.

I dug the money band out of the sack of clues. "My guess is that 'C.L.' and 'H.O.' are initials."

Andrea rolled her eyes. "Tell us something we don't know."

Really glad I didn't tell her about the dog.

"The money must've belonged to two people," I said, "since the initials are in different handwriting and different ink."

"What about the rubber stamp?" Chris asked.

"Yeah, well I don't exactly get that."

"It's like Gypsies use," Andrea said. "You know, like a hex to keep people from stealing the money."

"Gypsies don't use rubber stamps," I said. "Bankers or librarians but not gypsies."

Her lips tightened. "If you say so. Anyway, I'll have to work on it later. I have to go home now. Come on, Chris, let's go down to your place. I'll leave you a book, you can read some about fractions."

He made a face. "No way."

"Ms. Hendersen will be amazed."

"She'll be amazed I did my homework."

I gave Chris and Andrea the last two cookies and walked them to the door. I was kind of having fun and hated to see them go. Of course, Chris practically lived at my place. It was Andrea who wouldn't be around.

"Let's meet someplace Monday," I said.

She looked at me over her shoulder. "How about Pumperdingle's?"

I shot Chris a look. "Okay, but don't go by the Star market."

She stopped at the front door. "Why not? What's wrong with the Star market?"

Chris hadn't blabbed?

"We had some trouble there, that's all. You'd better get going or you'll be late."

"Okay, but be sure to bring your fingerprint set to Pumperdingle's. I'll have this figured out by then."

"*You* wish," I said.

I watched them walk down the hall talking to each other.

"Really?" she said, "The guy with all the tattoos?"

I shut the door. Thinking about Chockie made my stomach hurt. It hurt even worse when I remembered...

Day after tomorrow is Monday.

CHAPTER SEVEN
STUDENT MAN

I crawled out of bed feeling cheated. Sunday had shot by at the speed of light, and it was Monday, 6:45 a.m. Only two days in the weekend and I had goofed around and blown one.

I peeked outside. Dark, rainy, go-back-to-bed day.

Go ahead, play sick. Go back to bed.

But I couldn't. This was just the sixth week of middle school, I couldn't give up so soon. I pulled on my clothes, sucked down a bowl of gloppy cereal, and got into my rain coat.

Least Mom'll drive.

When I got to school I went to home room and tried to ditch my ugly mood. Nasty weather, leaf-clogged sewers, and if Chockie thought I'd sicked that dog on him, he'd probably kill me at about three-thirty. Still, it was time to pull myself together and be Student Man if only for my last day on earth.

I sat at my desk staring at my schedule like maybe that would change it. My absolute very least favorite class was gym, so, of course, it was first. On Tuesdays and Thursdays, my first class was good old art. But today wasn't Tuesday. Today was gym.

The rest of my schedule was the same for every day. Second hour, English, then social studies. Fourth hour, Spanish, then lunch. Fifth hour, computer lab; sixth hour, science; seventh hour, math.

During the first week of school, my math teacher, Mr. Abramovitz had told us about his Mystery Club. He said it would meet on Thursdays after school, and the first meeting had been scheduled for this week. He'd said the club members used deduction to solve their mysteries, and I knew from <u>Denison on Detection</u> and my other books that deduction was the method used by real detectives.

I had the trasher money band in my notebook and sneaked a peek.

Abramovitz'll know.

The announcements finally wound down, the bell rang, and we all headed for class. It was a long way to the gym, and I should have been hurrying, but I just couldn't force myself to. I'd have to undress to get into my gym stuff, and the guys would all look at my leg and my foot. I didn't even like looking at them, I sure didn't want them to.

Carlos Mendez had the locker next to mine. He was just pulling on his gym shirt when I got to my locker.

"Hi, Carlos."

"Oh, hi, Will, I thought they decided last week that you didn't have to take gym anymore."

I opened the door of my rusty old locker, threw in my book bag, and sat down on the long wooden bench. "I brought a note, but they said everybody had to take gym."

"Yeah, but I thought, you know, with your crippled foot..."

Crippled?

"It's not crippled, it's just a little weaker."

He looked at my shoe. "Yeah, sure. Sorry."

Gym wasn't so bad after all. I wore my sweat pants and, afterwards, I didn't take a shower. No one seemed to notice.

The rest of the morning was gray and dull, but by afternoon things improved. First there was computer lab, then science, then math. All my favorites.

I sat in computer lab waiting for my teacher, Ms. Pearson, and thought about the computer I was going to win from Andrea. Her rents would kill her, but it <u>was</u> her idea.

Hope they don't kill her too much.

Ms. Pearson entered the room just at the bell. Her face was thin and nervous like a hunted animal's. I wondered if I'd looked like that when Chockie chased me through Star Market.

Probably worse.

"Good afternoon, class," she said. "You may go on-line."

We turned on our computers. Ms. Pearson scooted to the far side of the room. "When your CPU boots be sure your PC's CRT is at the C prompt, then put your WIP floppy in the A drive."

I usually understood about half of her alphabet talk, but by being logical and by watching the kid next to me, I managed to compute. Today was different. My screen flashed, "NONSYSTEM DISC OR MEDIA, RETRY, IGNORE, ABORT."

I raised my hand and searched the room for Ms. Pearson. She had gotten clear to the back corner.

"Be right with you, William." Almost instantly she was.

"When your A drive is loaded with your WIP floppy prior to boot from the C drive," she said, "you must eject the A drive media, and reboot."

Whaa?

Her slender hands fluttered over the keyboard for a second, and the logo, IBM popped up. At least I hadn't wrecked the computer, but I had screwed up.

Modern detective science requires thorough familiarity with high-speed computers. -DENISON

Got to pay attention.

Science was after computer lab. Mr. Dirk was the teacher and he was the complete opposite of Ms. Pearson. Where Ms. Pearson was a moving target, Mr. Dirk usually just sat behind his desk twisting the ends of his feeble moustache or twirling his nerdy glasses by the ear piece.

Beyond clueless.

At his desk, as usual, Mr. Dirk leaned back in his chair, glasses spinning lazily. "Who did the reading for today?"

No hands.

He lowered his chair. "What *was* the reading for today?"

Silence.

Then I raised my hand.

"Mr. Wizard," he said.

I cleared my throat. "You didn't give us any reading for today. We still hadn't finished on the states of matter."

He looked drowsily around the room. "Is that right, Ms. Wizard?" he asked a girl in the front row.

"Yes, Mr. Dirk."

Like I'm gonna lie.

"Well," he said, "does anyone know anything about the states of matter?"

The rest of the class went about the same. This was Mr. Dirk's first year at Morrison, and I didn't care if it was his last. He was what Dad used to call a poor excuse for an officer. If we hadn't had such a good book I wouldn't have learned anything.

Math was the last class of the day, and Mr. Abramovitz was my favorite. He was smart and explained even hard things so you could understand.

At the end of class Mr. Abramovitz let us do our homework. I finished mine and still had about five minutes before class let out so I decided to reorganize my school stuff. I had a Science Fair notice from Dirk, but it was meant for eighth graders. There was a reminder that parent-teacher conferences would be held on Friday. I knew Mom wouldn't go. She hadn't been to a single conference since Dad died, but I didn't care, I was doing alright.

The bell rang and the class filed out. Kids laughed and shouted as they went to their lockers and headed home, but I was in no hurry to see if Chockie had figured out I wasn't at Parker Elementary anymore. I sat at my desk and waited for Mr. Abramovitz to finish his paperwork.

As I waited I kept my mind off of Chockie by practicing my detective skills on Mr. Abramovitz, like the Professor said.

A detective must be able to give a precise physical description of every person with whom he or she comes in significant contact. -DENISON

I figured Mr. Abramovitz was about six-two, middle-agey, forty-something. He was bald but combed a few wisps of black hair over the top. It looked pretty sad, but at least it was better than Dirk's road-kill toupee.

Mr. Abramovitz was thin, but had a round belly that made him look kind of like a tall spider, and his pale skin couldn't have been in the sunlight very often.

Definitely not athletic.

He was wearing a rumpled shirt and a short necktie that looked like a kid's clip-on. His shoes had probably never been polished, but it was his socks that were the weirdest. They didn't match, not even close. One was black nylon and had blue and white diamonds on the side. The other was maroon and woolly. My bachelor uncle, Phil was the last adult I'd seen wearing mismatched socks.

No wedding ring either...

"Is there something you wanted, Mr. Williamson?" Mr. Abramovitz had followed my stare down to his shoes and was lifting and sliding his feet trying to figure out what I was looking at.

"Huh? I mean, yes, I have something. Something that might be good for the club—for the Mystery Club."

"Let's have a look."

I went to his desk. "I found this, I mean a friend of mine did. It's a money band and it has this writing on it."

He inspected it briefly then reached into his desk and got a magnifying glass.

Detective?

He examined it for several minutes. "I don't think this is the kind of thing we can use. You see, Mr. Williamson, the Mystery Club is actually kind of a fraud. We don't work on real-life mysteries. Mostly, we work on numerical enigmas and mathematical conundrums."

He pulled his glasses halfway down his nose and held the money band at arm's length. "As for your money band, this writing '2m, H.O.' and 'C.L.' seems clear enough. '2m' is shorthand for two thousand and the money band is for a two thousand dollar stack. It appears to me that someone with the initials 'H.O.' counted the money and verified that there was two thousand dollars. The initials 'C.L.' are probably from another person who counted the money and then stamped over his initials with this 'W' seal to keep anyone from tampering with the counted money."

He pinned the band to his desk with a forefinger and looked at me over his glasses. "The 'Wraith' written on it here. That looks like a certain Mr. Williamson's hand writing."

The guy's good.

"It is my writing. I did it so I wouldn't forget. See the ring around the 'W' stamp?"

He used his magnifying glass again. "Ah, yes, I see. It's very small print. Does it say 'Wraith'?"

"Yes. I put it on my light box and—"

"You have your own light box?"

"My dad gave it to me."

"What model?"

"Lucas, LB-Forty-Two just like the Chicago Police Department uses."

"Multiple light source and variable intensity?"

"And colored jell inserts."

He took off his glasses, pulled out a shirt corner, and rubbed the lenses. "Excellent piece of equipment, first rate. I just use a window myself. Hold the subject material up to the glass and hope the sun's shinning. Lucas, eh?"

He handed the band back to me. "This 'Wraith', what do you suppose the meaning of that is?"

"It means a ghost, a specter, or phantom."

"Yes, but what do you suppose the *significance* of it is? It could be a company or perhaps a club. Can't say without more data." He put his glasses back on. "Tell you what, Mr. Williamson, bring this strip of paper back on Thursday. There are a couple of Mystery Club members who like this sort of thing, maybe we can do you some good. You were going to join, weren't you?"

"Yes, sir."

"Good. I've been looking at your test results. I think you'll like our little problems even if we can't help you with yours."

He turned the money band over one more time. "Found it in the trash, huh?"

"Yes, behind my building."

"Your *apartment* building?"

"Yes, sir."

"That is interesting." His bald head bobbed. "Quite interesting. Mind if I make a copy?"

"No, okay."

He got up, and I followed him down the hall to the media room. Several other teachers were milling about, talking, and putting assignments together. Mr. Dirk was there being "funny". When he saw Mr. Abramovitz his eyes lit up.

"Abra-halfwits, old boy. Got another live one for your Misery Club?"

Mr. Abramovitz walked by him without speaking. Mr. Dirk tossed a paper airplane at him. "Great tie. Did you buy it separately, or did it come with the jammies?" He giggled like a little kid. "Listen, Chuckster, don't take all day. I have some *real* work to do."

Mr. Abramovitz still said nothing. He made a quick copy and we went back to the math room.

"I'll work on this tonight," he said. "You might be able to find something in the library about the 'Wraith' clue. Ask the research librarian to run a scan on the word 'Wraith'. Her name is Ms. Scott, she knows me, so say I asked you to research it. I think there's a company called Wraith. Seems there was something in the news about it."

I was taking notes. Business or a place? Ms. Scott. I'd go to the library right after checking in with Captain Chris and Andrea.

"One other thing," he said. "After school the Mystery Club members all use first names. Call me Charlie, but only after school, right?"

"Yes, sir—Charlie."

He handed the money band back. I stuck it in my math book and headed for the side door. It had stopped raining and the weather had turned bright and cheerful. As far as I could see, the front sidewalk was clear of Vipers.

Could be hiding, like, in a doorway.

I thought about calling the cops. They knew about Chockie and they'd help the son of an ex-cop. But they'd tell Mom and she'd have a cow. I decided just to take the sidewalk across the middle of the park. At least no one could sneak up on me.

The park was pretty empty. The playground equipment was still wet from the rain so nobody was playing on it. There were two respectable looking people walking along the gravel exercise trail. Dorky Mr. Dirk was cutting across the soaking wet grass, ruining his shoes.

But no Vipers, no sweat.

I got to Pumperdingle's and spotted Andrea and Chris sitting in a booth in the back. Andrea waived. "Williamson, over here."

Chris scooted over and I sat.

"You want anything?" Andrea said, "I'm buying."

She's buying?

"Anything I want?"

"Anything that's less than boysenberry cheesecake."

"Then I think I'll have strudel. How about you, Chris? What're you getting?"

"I don't know. Not strudel, though. I still have some."

"Did you find anything out?" Andrea asked.

"Nothing much, but after here I'm going to the library. I want to look up 'Wraith' at the research desk. What'd you find out?"

"That's why we're celebrating," Chris said. "Andrea already knows about Wraith."

My chest tightened. "You mean you know who the trasher guy is?"

"No, but I'm close. My dad knew, he read it in the paper."

"Read what?"

"About Wraith. It's a holding company. I don't exactly know what that is. I think it just kind of owns things."

"The two thousand dollars belonged to it," Chris said.

"Probably," she said, "but that's not the best part. Dad said the FBI was investigating it for, like, *violent* crimes, and he said..."

She leaned closer.

"He said, two of their employees had been found in the river, shot in the head."

CHAPTER EIGHT
SOMETHING WICKED

I fished the money band out of my backpack. The filthy piece of trash wasn't part of a game anymore, it was a piece of something wicked. It could've been wrapped around some dirt bag's money just a week before. Maybe money from drug deals. Deals like the one Dad was investigating when he was killed.

I let the strip fall to the table and wiped my hands on my jeans.

"The bet's off. We have to take this to the cops. The FBI."

Andrea started to say something, but the waitress swooped down on the table and plopped a slice of boysenberry cheesecake in front of her.

"Decide whatcha want, hon?" the waitress asked Chris.

"Gimme a grilled cheese and a medium Coke."

The waitress scribbled on her pad and turned to me "How about you?"

"Nothing."

Chris almost dropped his water. "Nothing? Free eats and you don't want nothing?"

"Okay, a Coke."

The waitress flipped her pad shut and went to the kitchen. Andrea turned her plate around, sliced the tip off her cheesecake, swirled it in the purple pool of boysenberry sauce, and slipped it into her mouth.

How can she eat with that *thing* right there on the table?

The waitress zipped back through the kitchen door with our Cokes, "Grilled cheese'll be out in a sec, hon." then she disappeared again.

Andrea slooshed another bite of cheesecake in her boysenberry sauce. "If you're worried about losing your fingerprint set then we can call the bet off, but I started this and I'm going to finish it."

"*Worried?* I'm not—" I took a breath. "I'm not worried about the stupid bet, I'm worried about what's safe."

"Look at it the way the police would," she said. "The money band is just a piece of paper. So it has some writing on it, so big hairy deal. What could the cops do, grade the penmanship? Cops only have time for easy things, you know, obvious stuff. A clue like this is way too weird."

"It isn't weird. Mr. Abramovitz figured it out right away. Those initials are from the people who counted the money. One of them was paying the other in cash. That's how criminals work, cash only."

She sliced off another bite. "That's just your theory. Maybe the Wraith guys were victims, you know, like blackmail or kidnapping. I don't know what you're so hot about anyway. So long as we're the only ones who know about this we have nothing to worry about."

"Mr. Abramovitz knows," I said, "but I don't think he's a criminal. He wears clip-on ties."

"Well, don't go telling anybody else." She looked at Chris. "You haven't told anybody have you?"

His eyes were glued to the kitchen door. "No. Didn't what?"

"You didn't tell anyone about the money band?"

"Just you guys."

"Well, don't tell anyone else."

The waitress returned with Chris's grilled cheese sandwich. It looked good. Toasty brown on top with a couple of pickle spears on a piece of lettuce and a neat nest of potato chips. When its buttery smell reached my nose, I was kind of sorry I hadn't gotten more than just a Coke.

"You kids need anything else?" she asked.

"No thanks, hon," Andrea said. "Just the ticket."

The waitress scribbled on her little pad, tore off a sheet, and slapped it on the table.

We got quiet. Clattering plates and the mumble of the other customers were the only sounds. Then Chris started humming.

"Is it good?" Andrea asked.

"It's the best they have."

"You never got one before," I said.

"I get them sometimes. I don't do everything with you, you know."

"Ex-cuse me."

Andrea shifted uneasily in the booth. "I think I'd better pay. I have to be at my piano lessons at a quarter till five."

Piano?

"The heck with your piano lesson," I said. "We need to do something about this money band, right now."

"I want to think about your teacher's theory," she said. "Give me until Friday. If I can't come up with anything better by then, we can take it to the police."

"The FBI."

"The FBI." There was a boysenberry seed stuck between her front teeth. I guess I couldn't say no to a girl with a boysenberry seed in her teeth.

"Okay, until Friday, but call me if you find out anything before then. And thanks for the Coke."

"Yeah," Chris said, "thanks for the grilled cheese."

She put some change on the table and went to the front to pay. I checked to see if Chris was through. The ragged piece of lettuce was all that was left.

"You ready to go?"

"I guess so," he said. "Unless you want to split a cheesecake."

"Enough is enough."

"Okay, but let me finish my lettuce." He put a glob of ketchup on the lettuce leaf, rolled it up like a cigar, and ate it in one bite. "Dad says not to waste."

No danger of that.

We walked out of the deli into the bright afternoon sun. I was blinking against the light and thought I saw one of the Vipers standing in a doorway down from the deli. If he really was there, by the time my eyes got used to the light he was gone.

Back at home, I said goodbye to Chris and went up to my place. I didn't stay long though. I dropped off my books, picked up a half dozen detective posters, and left a note on the fridge.

"Mom. Went to the Adams Street Library. Back for dinner. -Billy."

Mom had always called me "Billy" and Dad, "William." All Dad's police friends called him Woody, but not Mom.

I got to the library without seeing any Vipers. I knew I'd be safe once I got inside. I'd never seen a Viper in the library.

Probably against their rules.

I went right to the reference section. That was where the encyclopedias were so I figured other research stuff must be close by. There was a horseshoe shaped counter in the middle of the section and a large man was sitting behind it, reading.

"Excuse me," I said, "I need the research desk."

He peered over his reading glasses. "History, government documents, newspaper-periodicals, fiction, or business?"

"I guess, business."

"This is business reference."

"Oh. Well I was kind of looking for," I checked my notes. "for Ms. Scott."

"Newspaper-periodicals, basement." He pointed to the back. "Through that door, down, follow the white line to the yellow line to the second desk on the right."

I scribbled the instructions. "White to yellow to second desk. Thanks."

The door the man had pointed to opened into a dark hall which led to a narrow set of stairs. I went down to the basement. Unlike the rest of the library, it wasn't carpeted and as I walked the sound of my shoes echoed off the concrete floor and walls. It sounded like an army was marching through the place, but it was just me.

Huge stale-smelling books filled the sagging shelves, and the bare bulbs that hung from the ceiling made a patchwork of light over the dingy stacks. I hurried along the white to the yellow line and down the yellow line, but there was no one at the first, second, or the third desk. I turned to follow the colored lines back upstairs and my clattering echoes returned.

I checked the signs on the ends of the rows as I walked. I was only half-interested in what they said. Mostly I just wanted something to keep my mind off how spooky it was.

One of the signs read, "Business Periodicals."

Maybe I can find something by myself.

I walked down the narrow hall of books reading titles as I went. "Annals of Cost Management Systems," "The American Society of Standard Measurement Weekly," "Journal of Monetary Crossover Evaluation." High on a top shelf I found a likely one called "Business Law Abstracts." I stood on my tip toes, pulled one of the heavy books out, and thumbed through several pages of charts and graphs. They meant absolutely nothing. I heaved the huge book back over my head and had it near the shelf when a woman spoke.

"We prefer to shelve..."

The book flipped out of my hands, and slammed into the concrete floor.

"Wham!" It echoed through the basement.

She had her hands to her face. "I'm *so* sorry, I didn't mean to startle you."

I dropped down, picked up the book, and with trembling hands held it out to her.

"I was trying to find something," I said. "I was supposed to see the second desk, I mean the second woman, but she wasn't there, I mean, Ms. Scott wasn't."

"I'm Ms. Scott. What did you need to see me about?"

My heart was still racing. "Mr. Abramovitz at Morrison Middle School said to."

"You're a friend of Chuck's?"

"Uh..."

"Well, if he wanted you to see me that's good enough. What did he want you to see me about?"

"He—we, I mean, *I* need to know about a company. I think the government is investigating it."

"A local company?"

"Yes."

"Then we can start with the newspapers. Follow me, I'll show you how we scan news stories."

I had a chance to calm down as I trailed her back to her desk, and I had a chance to scope her out.

She was wearing a necklace made of a child's toy block, a rabbit's foot, a wooden rhinoceros, and some green thing I didn't recognize. She had a single long brown braid that fell over the back of her loose overalls, and as soon as I looked at her feet I knew how she'd managed to sneak up on me. She was wearing fuzzy pink slippers with little bunny faces.

"I'll bet your feet get tired from these hard floors," I said.

"Oh." She turned toward me. "You mean my bunny-boys? Actually I wear them because they're quiet. This one," she raised her left foot, "is Chuck and this one is Max."

"Uh, hello."

"Oh, I don't think they're real, or anything."

Course not.

We got to her desk and she turned her computer on. A picture of a Japanese warrior flickered onto the screen with "Attack of the Samurai, II."

Game freak.

She quickly poked a key and the screen went to blue. "Now, what's the name of the company?"

"Wraith, it's spelled W-R-A-I-T-H. It's a holding company."

She typed "Wraith" followed by a series of numbers, pressed enter, and a list of titles appeared.

"There are twenty entries for local and seven for the national press," she said. "I'll print copies of the stories we have on the data base, and a list of the other articles by name and source."

When the printer finished rattling she tore off a stack of sheets and handed them to me. "I hope this is what you guys need. Tell Chuck not to be such a stranger. Okay?"

"Okay, and thanks, thanks a lot."

The city was redoing the outside of the library, and the construction company had put up a wooden tunnel to protect pedestrians from falling junk. I left the library with the print-outs and my posters and went into the dingy tunnel. About halfway through I found a nail head poking out. I pushed one of my posters against it so the nail popped through and held it in place.

A board creaked at the library end of the tunnel and I saw someone come in. I hurried out into the dim late-afternoon light and looked back. It was too dark to see who was there. I walked faster, glanced back—

Someone's coming. Running!

"Hey, kid!" It was a man's voice. I ran but got only a few steps before a heavy hand came down on my shoulder. I squirmed and tried to escape.

"Take it easy, kid."

I looked up to see who was holding me. It was a cop. He had my shoulder clamped in one hand and the poster I'd just put up in the other.

"No bills allowed."

"What?"

"No advertising on city property," he said.

"Oh, sorry."

"No sweat. Want to be a detective, huh?"

"Yes. Yes, sir."

"Rough job, detective."

"I know. My dad was a C.P.D. detective."

"Oh, yeah? What's his name?"

"Lieutenant Woody Williamson."

"You Woody's boy?"

"Yes, sir."

He smiled. "Well, small world. My sarge mentioned you at roll call. Said you were having trouble with the Viper street gang, that their leader was hassling you on account of your dad. I'm supposed to be keeping an eye on you. Guess I'm doing a good job."

Dad?

"What do you mean, on account of my dad?"

He tipped his cap back. "On account of your dad busted the creep's old man. I thought you knew."

"My dad busted Chockie's old—Chockie's dad?"

"Is that his name, Chockie?"

I nodded.

"Yeah, sorry, I thought you knew."

But I hadn't. I'd just figured Chockie was a natural creep.

"What did he bust him for?"

He thought for a minute. "Drug dealing, I think. Seems like his old man was a small-time pusher."

I'd never really thought about any of the kids of the people Dad busted. I still didn't know what to think. After all, he was only doing his job. It was sad for their kids, but it wasn't Dad's fault.

Not *my* fault either.

The cop patted me on the shoulder. "Anyway, Sarge said we wouldn't have to worry about this Chockie jerk for a while."

"How come?"

"He's in the hospital. Some kid sicked a dog on him."

CHAPTER NINE
SOMETHING NEAR

Rumors! How could a cop help spread lies like that? I hadn't sicked the dog on Chockie, Chockie knew that. At least I hoped he did, because if he thought I <u>made</u> it attack him—

This whole thing was getting out of hand.

I mean, why did Chockie want to get me anyway? He had no reason to hate me, Dad was just doing what the city wanted. What was Chockie going to do, get even with the whole city?

Yeah, probably the whole city.

I guess he especially hated Dad, but that was just dumb. He'd probably never even met him. If he had, he couldn't have hated him. Dad was just Dad. There to listen, to help, to hug, and fix it. It didn't matter to him that he was around crooks most of the time. He treated them the same as he treated Mom and me. It even got him in trouble sometimes. Mom would say he was giving half his salary to the families of the dopers he'd busted.

"Only a few people are naturally bad," he'd say, "We have to get them off the street, but we don't want their families to suffer any more than they already have."

That was Dad. Naturally good.

I can remember the last time I saw him like it was this morning. I'd finished my breakfast and was going out the door to school. "Meet you at the park after school," he said. But he wasn't at the park, and when I got home I knew by the way Mom was crying that I would never see him again.

"Killed in the line of duty," the paper said, but was there any duty worth the loss of my dad, my best friend?

If only Chockie had known him.

Somewhere down an alley a dog barked and I shuddered. I was living more and more in fear and I didn't like it. I remembered how afraid I'd been as I hurried home from school. All the while Chockie had been on his back in a hospital somewhere.

Did the cop say where? No.

I'd had enough. I was through with running. Panicking and running out the back door of the grocery had certainly been a stupid move even though I'd managed to escape. I couldn't run forever. Sooner or later the Viper's would catch me or I'd hurt myself running.

That's it. No more.

I'd avoid the Vipers when I could, but if I had to, I'd face them and Chockie. I'd tell them I was innocent; that I'd done nothing.

Overhead, a street light blinked and tried to come on.

Vipers rule the night.

I picked up my pace and got back to Park Manor just as the cold and the dark closed over the city. Mother was on the couch in the living room. She was reading the paper, but I knew she'd already fixed dinner. I could smell it and it smelled good.

"Hi, Mom."

"Hi, Billy. How was the library? Did you get your homework done?"

"I did it at school, I was working on a project."

I wanted to say I'd been tracking dangerous criminals, but I knew better. Dad had been a great detective, even decorated for valor, but Mom would never have agreed to let me follow in his footsteps.

"If the pushers can't buy a cop they kill him," she'd say, "so don't expect a bunch of crooked cops to catch the scum that killed your father. They're all in it together. Stay away from all of them."

It hurt me that she hated the police. When she raked the good guys, it was like she was killing Dad again. Like he hadn't died enough.

I leaned back against the wall and watched her curled up on the couch, reading the evening paper. She looked so small, almost like a little girl. It was easy to see why people sometimes thought she was my sister instead of my mom, But she'd been the boss of the family when Dad was alive and she still was. Eventually she'd find out. She'd see one of my posters or someone would blab.

She put the paper down. "You got a call from some man named Hope and from a lady. The numbers are on the pad in the kitchen."

"Is it okay if I call the lady back before dinner?"

"I suppose so. Do you know what she wants?"

"Oh, I'm just trying to get some odd jobs. You know, spending money."

"Well, she did seem anxious to talk to you. We can eat when you get through."

"What's for dinner?"

"Stew and biscuits."

I liked Mom's stew even though we had it a lot. It was cheap to make and we had to watch our money.

I went down the hall to the kitchen to get my messages. It smelled even better in there. I snuck the lid off the stew pot and took a peek.

Potatoes, onion, and carrots. Big pieces, too.

"Stay out of the stew," Mom called from the living room, "and wash your hands."

She's the detective.

I picked up the message pad. "Mrs. Archibald Vanderbur, 555-2326/ Mr. Noah Hope about some copy machine?"

I punched in the woman's number. After a couple of rings, a man answered.

"Vanderbur residence," he said, in an English accent.

"This is WW Williamson. I'm a detective. May I speak with Mrs. Vanderbur, please?"

"Certainly, sir. One moment, please."

I liked the way he'd said that. I wondered if I could talk that way.

Suttanly, suh. One moe-munt, plee-uz.

Mrs. Vanderbur came on the line. "Is this the young man who advertises as a detective?"

"This is WW Williamson, and I've put up some posters about my detective agency. May I help you?"

"Oh, my, such a mature well-mannered young man. You may indeed help me, that is, if you can. I saw your advertisement and I thought your age would be an advantage. You see my nephew, Melrose, is staying with me for a few months, and I am afraid he is not very happy with the arrangement. I've tried to talk to him about what might be wrong, but I can't seem to get through. I'd like you to look into the matter for me and see if you can determine what the problem is."

Melrose? That's the problem.

"Yes, ma'am, I'm sure I can help. When would you like me

to start?"

"He's at an asthma clinic this week having some diagnostic tests done. We'll have to wait for his return."

"That's okay," I said, "I'm working on another case now anyway. I should be finished with it by next week."

"Another case? What sort of case is it? If I may be so bold."

"I'm not really sure yet. It may be nothing, but it may be big."

"I see. But you will have time for my little matter?"

"Yes, ma'am."

"Splendid. Then I'll call you as soon as Melrose returns. Should I send you a retainer check?"

"No, it's ten dollars, but only if I can help."

"Ten dollars an hour seems a very reasonable rate. Of course if you have any expenses I'll reimburse you, and my car and driver will be at your disposal. The important thing is to help Melrose. Agreed?"

I cleared my throat to keep from choking. "Yes, sure. Good-bye, Mrs. Vanderbur."

"Until then, dear boy."

I had to sit down.

Ten dollars an hour!

"Mom! This lady's going to pay me ten dollars an hour. I said ten dollars and she thought I meant an hour."

Mom hurried down the hall to the kitchen. "What on earth does she want you to do for ten dollars an hour?"

"Just talk to some kid and see why he's not happy."

"You sure it wasn't just one of your friends pulling a joke?"

"No, it's really real. I think she's, like, rich. This English guy answered the phone, and she has a car she *sends* places."

"That's pretty rich. When we send the car we have to go along, and we don't have any Englishman to answer our phone."

"Oh, but suttanly we do," I said, and we laughed. We laughed harder than we had for a long time.

All the good news made dinner that night taste even better, and the stew seemed to have more meat than usual.

After dinner I rinsed the dishes and put them in the dishwasher. Mom went to the living room with her glass of booze. We called it wine, but it was booze, gin. We'd had such a good time when we were laughing that I'd hoped she'd skip it just this once.

The dishwasher startled me when it kicked in with a

whoosh. I left it to do its work and went to my room. The big pile of computer printouts was waiting for me. Maybe I could get my mind off the gin by reading about somebody else's troubles.

The first article Ms. Scott had found was about six months old. It was the Wraith company's annual report and it looked pretty boring. I was about to skip it when I spotted something interesting. The top of the second page had the full name of the company, Wraith, Limited. and a copy of their logo, a circled W just like the one that was stamped on the trasher money band.

I highlighted the logo with my marker and moved on. The next story was over nine months old and proved that Mr. Braintree had been right about Wraith. The FBI was investigating it.

Local Firm Implicated in Weapons Smuggling Case

Federal investigators reportedly have uncovered a plot involving Wraith, Ltd., of suburban Des Plaines, and German factions of The International Army of Liberation, an avowed terrorist organization. A highly placed FBI source said persons connected with Wraith, Ltd., had attempted to exchange a large supply of automatic weapons and military style explosives for cash and narcotics.

Wraith, Ltd., was incorporated in Delaware in 1990 and purportedly operated as a real estate holding company. Attempts to contact the company have been unsuccessful.

*****

There were lots of other articles that said about the same thing, but one had something new.

Millions Unaccounted for in Local Case

Federal investigators working on the Wraith, Ltd., weapons smuggling case have uncovered a scheme used to embezzle millions of dollars from the company. FBI agents said the missing funds were unrelated to the original investigation and that the company appears to have been the victim of employee theft. Agents said that from November to December of last year over three million dollars in cash and bearer bonds had been stolen.

Informed sources said that Carl LePonte, the company's former chief financial officer, left the company's employ in December, and that his current whereabouts are unknown. Neither the FBI nor company officials would confirm whether or not LePonte is a suspect in the thefts.

*****

I read it three times and tried to imagine what kind of guy would steal from a bunch of drug pushers and gun smugglers.

Tough, like Chockie, but smart, like Mr. Abramovitz.

I looked back at some of the other clippings and thought about Chris's trasher and about the money band. The "C.L." on it certainly matched up with Carl LePonte. But was Braintree right? Was there too little hard evidence for the police to be interested?

Decisive action, that was the last step in the Detective's Credo. I was ready to act on Chockie and the Vipers, was it time to act on Wraith too? I checked my list of evidence one last time.

1. Wraith is really a bunch of dope pushers and gun smugglers
2. Their money guy stole millions from them
3. The money band had Wraith's stamp on it and it was in the building trash container
4. The janitor never lets anyone else dump anything in our trash container, and he wouldn't bother to pick up stuff from anywhere but the building

Conclusion: One of the Wraith guys (probably, Carl LePonte) ripped off his gangster pals, and now he probably lives right here in the building.

Tomorrow, I'd talk to Mr. Abramovitz, Braintree too. This wasn't a game anymore. There was something evil in the building, something dangerous, something near.

CHAPTER TEN
THE SILENT VICTIM

Tuesday morning I was running late for school. I hustled across the park wondering if other detectives had to sweat tardy slips. I got to home room right at the bell, and the morning announcements were droning over the intercom. Something about the Fall Festival, as if I cared, and a reminder that discount art supplies were still available—

Art? Oh, no, I was supposed to bring something.

But before I could think of what it was, the bell rang and I headed for the art room.

A guy named Steve sat next to me in art. When I got to class, he was in his seat, talking to the girl in front of him. "My mom said I used to stick mine in my mouth."

She made a face. "Well, mine are coated with plastic. Mom said I'd want them when I get older."

"Who'd want smelly old baby shoes?"

Baby shoes...

He turned to me. "Did you forget your baby shoes?"

"No. I, uh, I never had any."

That was true. I'd spent the first five years of my life in braces and casts. Even if Mom had saved one of my braces I wouldn't have wanted to bring it.

"No sweat," he said, "you can use one of mine. Ms. Day only said we had to bring a shoe she didn't say we had to bring two. We can just say we only had one each when we were little, and that we used to hop a lot."

"Yeah, you hopped on your right and I hopped on my left. Thanks, man."

He handed me one of his little white shoes. I held it in the palm of my hand. It was perfect, like it had never been worn.

Ms. Day came in and the class quieted down. Our first project was to sketch our baby shoe. She said it was a study of human anatomy. I tucked my feet under my chair.

Grim as it was, I managed to survive the rest of art and laid low in English and social studies. By the time sixth-hour bell rang, I'd gone over the Wraith case in my mind hundreds of times. I hurried from science to the math room and got there just as the last kid was leaving. Mr. Abramovitz was sitting at his desk.

"Well, Mr. Williamson. Did you get over to see Ms. Scott at the library?"

"Yes, and she found some great stuff on Wraith."

"Wraith? That's what was written on the money band?"

"It's a company and—"

"Not now. See me after class."

All class long I squirmed in my seat dying to tell him about the thieves and drug pushers and about how I'd tracked one of them to my building.

He passed down the aisle and suddenly stopped beside me. "Mr. Williamson, define 'integer' for me."

Integer? What does that have to do—

"Well, Mr. Williamson?"

"It's a number."

"Is seven hundred an integer?"

"Yes."

"Is one and one half an integer?"

"Yes."

The smart girl in the front row raised her hand and waved it.

"I mean, no."

"Why not?"

"Because..."

Her hand shot up again.

"Because an integer is a whole number."

"Correct," he said, "I'm glad to see you are paying attention."

After that I listened more carefully, and that seemed to make class drag on forever. When the bell finally rang I packed up my books and lined up last at Mr. Abramovitz's desk. The kids ahead of me had questions about their homework or some other dumb thing. I waited as patiently as I could. I had my computer printouts so I sorted through them for the millionth time. Finally my turn came.

"Well, I see Ms. Scott loaded you down with output," Mr. Abramovitz said.

"Uh-huh, Wraith is a company, and it has the exact same

logo of a circled W as the money band, and the FBI is investigating it which must mean one of the Wraith people lives in my building because one of them stole some money, and that's how the money band got in the trash and that explains..."

He held up his hands. "Whoa, wait just a minute. Let's look at the printouts and see what we can agree on."

I handed him the printouts and he sorted through them. Every once in a while he'd frown or grunt, but he didn't say anything.

After about ten minutes he set the pile down. "So, the way I see it, the Wraith company was accused of gun running and drug dealing, but they were also the victim of what appears to be embezzlement."

"That's right, and I think the money band was wrapped around some of the money that was embezzled from Wraith. I figure the guy who stole the money lives in my building and he threw the money band away to get rid of evidence."

"You keep saying 'he.' What makes you think our suspected embezzler is male?"

"The newspaper said Carl LePonte used to be the main money-guy for Wraith, and that he disappeared about the time they found out the money was missing."

"Yes, the newspaper article said that, but it didn't draw any conclusions. Careful people like reporters, detectives and mathematicians don't operate on guesses. We're precise or we're nothing, right?"

Exactly like the professor.

Precision is the detective's minimum standard. - DENISON

"You're right," I said. "I was being sloppy."

"Not to worry. That's why we have math class. I catch you, you catch me, together we think clearly."

He thumbed through the pile of computer printouts and reread a couple of them. "I think it's too early to draw any conclusions as to whom the thief is, but the C.L. initials on the money band certainly match Carl LePonte. Of course he <u>was</u> Wraith's financial officer, so he would legitimately handle money, still I think we should show your evidence to the police. It'd probably be best if I did the talking. They might take an adult more seriously."

"Shouldn't we tell the FBI? They're the ones who are investigating Wraith."

He was separating the printouts into several piles and he looked up. "FBI? I suppose you're right. This is a federal matter. Let's go to the office. We can call from there."

It was getting late and there were only a few people in the office. Mr. Abramovitz sat at an empty desk, looked up the number of the FBI, and called.

"May I speak with someone concerning the Wraith, Limited, gun smuggling and drug case?" He drummed his fingers on the desk. "Hello, my name is Charles Abramovitz. I'm calling from the Morrison Middle School here in Chicago. I have some information that might be of interest to you in your investigation of Wraith, Limited—No, Wraith, W-R-A-I-T-H. Yes, that's right, gun running and drug trafficking. I have some information that— What? Oh, I see." He put his hand over the phone's mouthpiece. "The case is closed."

He went back to the phone. "Actually the information we have is related to the embezzlement of funds from Wraith rather than directly to the smuggling case. Uh-huh, yes. Well, thank you anyway." He hung up. "The agent said the embezzlement case is the responsibility of the Des Plaines police."

He looked up a number in one of the suburban directories, and called. "I'd like to speak with the department that's handling the Wraith, Limited, embezzlement case, please. No, that's Wraith, W-R-A-I-T-H. Yes, I'll hold." He rolled his eyes. "The run around."

"Hello, my name is Charles Abramovitz and I have some information on the—Yes, I'll wait."

"My name is Charles C. Abramovitz, I'm a math teacher at Morrison Middle School here in Chicago, and one of my students found some interesting evidence that I think you could use in the Wraith, Limited, embezzlement case. He found a money band which has the stamp of—Yes, Wraith, Limited. It was in the Des Plaines paper on..." He looked at me.

"January fifth," I said.

"Last January fifth, and I wanted—There isn't? No one? No, not right now, but if I do, what's your name? Okay, thanks."

He hung up and sat with a puzzled look on his face. "That's odd."

"What'd he say?"

"She said there was no case open on the Wraith embezzlement. No one ever filed a complaint."

"No one?"

He twisted the phone cord around his finger and gazed out the window. "Even though they lost over three million dollars the people at Wraith were unwilling to make a complaint."

He looked at me. "Tell me, William. Why do you suppose Wraith wouldn't want the police involved?"

"Well, if they really are a bunch of gangsters, they probably don't much like cops. Besides, maybe they want to catch the guy, themselves."

He raised an eyebrow. "Villains stalking a villain. Hmm, if that's true, I wonder if they're close."

CHAPTER ELEVEN
THE GLASS LIZARD

Mr. Abramovitz sat at the desk looking even more like a teacher than usual. "This business is taking on a pretty bad odor. How many of your friends did you say know about it?"

"Just two."

"Well, two's too many. These Wraith people are involved in drug trafficking and gun running, and those are especially heinous crimes. I think I'd better take the information you and Ms. Scott found to a fellow I know at the police department."

Maybe a friend of Dad's.

"Is he a detective?"

"No, computer specialist, but he's close to a lot of investigations. He'll know why the FBI closed their case. At the very least, he'll be able to light a fire under the Des Plaines police. In the meantime I don't want you kids checking out any of these leads, understand? You might run into our embezzler; maybe even the Wraith goons."

I sat on the cold edge of the steel desk and thought about my promise to Andrea. I had said I'd wait until Friday to go to the police. Of course, I hadn't promised not to talk to my math teacher. He was the one who'd decided to call the cops, not me.

Mr. Abramovitz stood and gathered his notes. "I think your theory is very likely to prove correct, and if a person who was bold enough to embezzle millions of dollars from dangerous criminals <u>is</u> living in your building I don't think he or she should be messed with, do you?"

I ran my hand back and forth on the desk's smooth surface. "I wasn't messing with anything, Mr. Abramovitz."

"Charlie, remember, it's Charlie, after hours, and 'messing' was a poor choice of words. The work you've done is better than the FBI or the Des Plaines police have managed. What I meant was, young people like you are vulnerable. Adults have the upper hand to begin with, and an adult who's cunning enough to steal from dangerous criminals and then clever enough to hide right under their noses is an expert at manipulation and deceit. He could be anyone. I mean, he or *she*—I wish we knew this jerk's name."

"My dad used to make up code names for crooks when he didn't know their real name," I said. "There was this Canadian drug smuggler he called Cold Front."

"Your father was a policeman?"

"He's dead but, yeah."

"Oh, I am sorry." He leaned over the desk and patted my shoulder. "Well, if policemen use code names, I guess we should too. How about, 'Chameleon'?"

Chameleon?

"You mean, like the tea?"

He chuckled. "It's chamomile tea. Don't you people learn anything in Mr. Dirk's science class?"

"If it's in the book."

"Well, a chameleon is a lizard; a lizard that can change its color. If there were one on your sleeve its skin would change to the brown and green of your shirt making it as invisible as if it were made of glass. The only way you would be able to see it is if the light were just right."

"What does the light have to do with it?"

"You tell me. The light would make, what?"

"Oh, a shadow. It'd make a shadow."

"Exactly, a shadow can be seen even when its owner can't, and isn't that what's happened here?"

He propped his right elbow in his left hand the way he did when he was explaining a math problem. "Consider the facts. Number one, Chameleon ripped off this Wraith company. As I say, that's pretty gutsy since they're a pack of cold-blooded thugs. Number two, Wraith is just a few miles from here. If you were running from a bunch of unhappy hoods, wouldn't you go to Australia or some other far away place?"

"Far away as I could."

"Most people would, but Chameleon is counting on the ability to hide right under their noses; to blend in. Could even be your next-door neighbor. That's why I don't want you kids on this case anymore."

"But we can help you catch him, I mean, Chameleon. I have some ideas about who he is."

"He or she. You keep forgetting. We need precise thinking. Embezzlement is a crime commonly committed by both men and women."

"I know, I know. It's just that Carl LePonte disappearing like he did sure makes him look guilty. Besides, all the bad guys I ever met were boys—or men."

A secretary was the only other person still in the office. She stood by the office door tapping her foot and staring at us. Mr. Abramovitz didn't seem to notice.

"Man or woman," he said, "we're dealing with a desperate and cunning individual. I'll be sure you and your friends get the credit. You figured it out, now it's time to pass this on to the police."

The secretary cleared her throat and jiggled her keys. He finally noticed. "Better get out of here. Need a ride?"

"No, thanks. I want to stop off and see my friend. I need to warn her."

"Good. I'm glad we're in agreement. See you tomorrow, and don't worry. We'll figure out a way to get the police interested."

I left the office and went down the long hall to my locker. I worked the combination and jerked the handle. The door swung open and a note fluttered out.

Chockie sayd to keep an eye on you that nobudy gets you. We was watching for you even when you dint see us. Chockie says he personly take care of you hiself when he get out the hospitel.

At the bottom was a bloody smear in the shape of a snake.

I wadded it up , threw it on the floor, and shot a glance down the hall to the side door.

They're probably waiting for me.

I snuck down the hall, went out the side door, and crouched by the corner of the steps, checking the street. Several kids I didn't recognize were hanging around. A few of the bigger ones looked tough enough to be Vipers.

I decided I'd better take Mr. Abramovitz up on his ride offer, but his car pulled out of the teachers' lot and disappeared down the street.

I knew I couldn't stay crouched on the stairs much longer. Even if the tough looking kids weren't Vipers, they'd be sure to pick on me if they noticed me acting weird. But what else could I do?

Wait and call Mom when she gets home from work.

But I'd never done that before, and she'd have had a million questions. Of course, I could always walk home, but the Vipers would be expecting that. Or I could go to Andrea's, warn her about the Wraith business, and kill time until Mom could come get me.

Andrea's place seemed like the best bet, if only I could get past the tough kids milling around on the sidewalk. I took a deep breath and went down the stairs. They stopped talking as I got near and split into two groups. I couldn't go around, I'd have to go through.

Each wobbly step came hard, like walking on a trampoline. Any moment, a big hand would come smashing down on my shoulder.

Don't look up at them.

But I guess they weren't in a bullying mood. I slid by, close enough to touch, but they didn't so much as shuffle their feet.

It took half a block for the hair on my neck to lie down. I picked up my pace, and in a few minutes was pushing through the front door of Andrea's place, headed for the elevators.

"One moment." It was the woman at the front desk. "Are you expected?"

"Yes, Andrea, Andrea Braintree. She knows me."

"Whom shall I say is calling?"

Whom?

"William Wordsworth Williamson, the third."

She picked up a phone, spoke briefly and hung up. "If you would have a seat in the vestibule, Ms. Braintree will receive you shortly."

In the what?

At least I understood the have-a-seat part so I went back to the lobby and sat. The chair I picked looked ordinary enough, but when I flopped down on it I almost sank out of sight in its stuffing. This was definitely better than the Salvation Army rejects in the lobby of my place.

It felt real good to get off my feet. I usually put them up as soon as I got home. I could make it through the school day, but then I usually needed rest.

"Mr. Williamson?" The lady was leaning over the front desk so she could see me.

"Yes?"

"Ms. Braintree will see you now. Level thirty-seven, suite C."

Just when I was getting comfortable.

I struggled up from the chair and crossed the lobby to the elevator banks. I got in the elevator and when it took off, my right leg buckled and I had to steady myself against the wall.

Andrea's was waiting at her apartment door. "Hi, WW, hope you brought your fingerprint set."

She had on a frilly blouse. Her hair was on top of her head and tied with a silk scarf. I walked past her into the front hall and caught a whiff of perfume.

Definitely roses.

We went into the living room and I got a whiff of something else. People who have cats sometimes have that problem and Andrea had a big cat. Felicity was her name, but I had always called her Ferocity because she bit. She'd nailed me on the ankle the last time I'd been in their old apartment.

Watch where you sit.

Andrea patted the back of the sofa. "Have a seat. I'll be right back."

She darted down the hall and returned in a flash, waving a piece of paper and singing, "I know, I know, I know how we can solve the tra-sher."

She sat next to me and dropped a piece of paper in my lap. "My dad gave me the idea. You remember this photocopy I made of the cleaner's claim check? Well, I told Dad about it, and he said you could make the cleaners pay for your lost clothes or make them get your clothes back from the person they gave them to."

"What do you mean *I* could?"

She waved her hand lightly. "I mean, I told him it was your claim check."

"I see, so you want me to go to the laundry and pretend the claim check was mine?"

"Right, and when they can't find the clothes, you make a stink and say you want to know who took them. They're bound to have that in their records."

"Good idea," I said. "You go."

"I can't. I was already there once, remember? It has to be you. But I still win because it's my plan."

"I can't pretend the clothes are mine," I said. "That's illegal."

"How? You wouldn't really take them. The worst it could be is snoopy. Isn't it worth a little snoopy to find out who the trasher person is?"

Stalking, like the hoods from Wraith.

"Listen," I said, "I told you I showed the trasher stuff to Mr. Abramovitz, my math teacher. Well, he agrees that we're dealing with dangerous people, and he kind of called the cops and the FBI."

She jumped to her feet. "He *what?* You said we wouldn't go to the police until Friday! We were going to give it until Friday!"

I waited until she stopped stomping around. "Look, I know we were going to wait, but that's why I came over. I wanted to tell you about these newspaper stories I found at the library. Your Dad was right about Wraith. The trasher stuff Chris found belonged to this criminal we're calling Chameleon. That's his code name. I mean, it's his or her code name. It's like the lizard that can change color."

She just stared out the window.

Thinking? Mad? *Scared?*

She took the claim check and looked at it. "I have an idea. Their phone number's on here somewhere."

She picked up the phone and called. "Hello, I'm so sorry to bother you, but I came across a claim check for some of my cleaning. It's several weeks old, and I was wondering if my husband had picked it up. Could you? Yes, the number is I C one six five H, thank you, dear." She put her hand over the phone. "She's checking."

"Checking what?"

She held a finger to her lips to shush me, then went back to her conversation. "Oh, yes, happily married for over a year, now. He did? Well, that is such a relief, you'll never know. Yes, that would be nice. Thank you so much."

She hung up and looked at me like she'd been elected kid-of-the-year.

"Well," I said. "What did they say?"

"She said the laundry was picked up in August."

"But we already knew that. Did she tell you who picked it up?"

"Not in so many words, but she did say she didn't realize Milt was married."

"Milt? Milt who?"

"That's the best part. Just before she hung up she said, 'Hope to meet you real soon, Mrs. Katz.'"

CHAPTER TWELVE
A DEVIOUS NEIGHBOR

Katz!

Of course, it had to be my neighbor, Mr. Katz. That phony looking beard, the way he fumbled with his crutches. He had to be Chameleon.

Andrea sure looked proud of herself, and she had every right to. She was the true detective. She deserved to win my fingerprint set.

"It was kind of funny," she said. "The lady told me her husband was always losing his claim checks, too. Made me feel like I really was some dork's wife."

"That was really awesome," I said. "But how did you know it was a man who lost the claim check?"

"I didn't. It's just I can only do a woman's voice so I had to be a wife. The lady at the cleaners just assumed I was Ms. Katz."

"We have to tell Mr. Abramovitz," I said. "He can have him arrested."

She looked at me like she thought I was brain damaged. "We can't have him arrested if we don't know where he lives."

"But we do. You *met* him. Remember last week when we were at my place, and a guy on crutches came down in the elevator? That was Mr. Katz."

"*Milt* Katz?"

"Milt, Milton. Same thing."

She sat on the arm of the couch, a knuckle pressed to her lips. "I wonder if it's the right guy."

"Sure, I see him all the time. He lives right down the hall."

"I mean, I wonder if Katz is the right guy."

"Sure he is. Didn't you say that the lady at the cleaners— Oh, I see. You mean because he uses crutches."

"No, I—"

"Because he's just a cripple."

"No, I don't—"

I jumped up from the couch. "Yes you do. You think if he isn't *normal* then he can't do anything or be anybody. It's just like Chockie. Think you're better than somebody just because—"

She hopped up and took hold of my arm. "Look, I'm sorry, okay? I was thinking Mr. Katz didn't look like a criminal, but it wasn't because of his crutches. Well, maybe it was, but that's just stupid me. I didn't mean to hurt your feelings. I've always thought you were special. And I know handicapped people can do anything the rest of us can."

Handicapped?

Was that how she saw me? I'd thought she was getting softer, sweeter.

But it was only sympathy; sympathy and apologies.

"You don't have to apologize. I know I'm different, I get reminded every time I get dressed. It's my problem, I've got to deal with it."

"But it's not like that at all. Don't you remember when we used to play? I'd always want to be just like you, do everything you did?" She brushed her fingers down the back of my hand. "Remember? Your dad called me Little Shadow."

I remembered, and for a second I could see that little shadow in her grown-up face.

"We solved this together," she said. "I just got lucky with the cleaners' thing. Of course you're right about Katz. I'm sorry I hurt your feelings."

She looked like she meant it. I took a deep breath and the anger inside me started to spin down. "Okay—alright, I'm sorry, too. Shouldn't be so touchy. Temper's a waste."

She sat back down on the sofa and picked up the telephone. "Why don't we call your Mr. Abramovitz right now."

"No, what you said yesterday was right. We need to have lots of evidence to get the police interested. I'd better check up on Katz a little more."

She leaned toward me. "We'll both do it."

"No, it's too dangerous."

She took the phone from her lap and slapped it down on the coffee table hard enough to make the receiver bounce off. "<u>Don't</u> tell me it's too dangerous for a girl."

"It's not that, It's only I—" A last bright ray of the setting sun lit up the room and changed her hazel eyes to green. "I just don't want you hurt."

A jingling scratchy sound came from the back of the apartment.

She shot a look over her shoulder. "Mom's at the back door."

"Yeah, uh, I'd better go; better call home."

She handed me the phone and I called. Mom said she'd be right over. Could I wait at the street?

Andrea walked me to the door. "Don't do anything about Katz without telling me."

"I won't," I said, but I knew I would never put her in danger. I rode down in the elevator and waited out front, close to the door.

I was day dreaming, I guess, or Mom knew a short cut because, before I knew it, she was pulling up to the curb.

"Hi, Billy. Busy day?"

"Yeah."

"Tired?"

"Sort of."

We drove the rest of the way home in silence. When we pulled into the parking garage, I asked Mom to let me out at the back door. I shuffled up the ramp that ran beside the stairs and waited while she parked.

A red sports car snarled into the garage and whooshed by a few feet from the ramp. It was the flashy kind of car dope pushers drove on tv. I could almost hear machine gun fire; Wraith's hit man gunning me down.

I knew it was only the lady in the penthouse, but any day now—

Precision.

I could hear Mr. Abramovitz's warning. I needed precision, not panic. I needed to pull the case together, but something was resisting. Something wasn't right.

What? What doesn't fit?

Crimes had been committed, the paper proved that, and there were victims, but—

Of course. How could I forget?

The thugs at Wraith had never filed a complaint. Katz was an embezzler, alright, but there was nothing the police could do, and the FBI would only go after him for a federal crimes.

But Professor Denison said the feds used tax laws to nail thieves. Katz wouldn't have stolen three million dollars from the thugs at Wraith just to turn it over to the government.

"Are you sure you're alright?" Mom's voice made me jump about half a foot in the air.

"What? Yeah, fine."

"You sure nothing happened at school?"

I shrugged and pulled the door open and headed to the elevators.

On the way up, I remembered Chris. Whether we could make a case against Katz or not, at least Chris had to be warned there was a dangerous criminal in the building.

I pushed the third floor button. "I need to stop off at Chris' for a second."

"They're probably eating, you'd better wait until after supper."

The elevator door slid open. "They always eat late. I'll be up in a second."

I went down the hall and rang Chris's bell. Mr. Hebert answered. He was holding a napkin.

"WW, how's the lad?"

"Fine, Mr. Hebert. Sorry to bother you while you're eating, but I need to talk to Chris."

"Sure, come on in." He turned and yelled down the front hall. "Chris! WW's here."

Chris zipped around the corner, pulling a napkin from his shirt. "I called a hundred times, but you weren't there."

"Sorry, but listen..." I waited until Mr. Hebert was around the corner. "Andrea found out who the trasher dude is, it's Mr. Katz."

"From upstairs?"

"Yeah. That cleaners' claim check in the trasher stuff belonged to him."

"How do you know?"

"Andrea called the cleaners. It was beautiful—really beautiful. But, uh, be careful. Katz is a very dangerous guy."

"He doesn't look dangerous."

"Listen, I'm telling you he's the one. He's dangerous. If you aren't careful he'll <u>get</u> you."

He shrank back against the wall. "Okay."

"I'm sorry, I didn't mean to scare you. I just don't want you hurt. Katz is like a chameleon, he can look like anything he wants to. He may not even need those crutches."

"Chameleon?"

"Yeah, this lizard that can change color and disappear.

That's our code name for him. 'Chameleon.'"

His eyes got real big. "Is he a gangie?"

"Like a gangie."

"I'll call the cops and tell them he killed someone. They'll come like the last time."

"Last time they didn't catch anybody, remember? But don't worry. We'll call the cops, just not yet. Right now you need to be careful. Don't say anything to anybody, and stay away from Katz."

"I'll pretend I'm sick and stay home," he said.

"No, go to school, you'll be safe there. Teachers are trained for this kind of stuff." I gave him a playful punch on the arm.

"Now, I got to go. See you tomorrow," I said, and went upstairs.

Dinner was on the table. It was leftovers. I chewed on a dried-up lima bean and tried to block out the morons screaming on Mom's tv game-show.

A disgusting denture commercial came on. Mom hit the mute and turned to me. "You're sure quiet tonight, Billy. Is there something you need to talk about?"

I stirred my nuked potatoes. There was lots I wanted to say—"Aw, those twits get so excited over a stupid game. You'd think being on some stupid tv show was the only important thing." That wasn't it.

She raised the remote. "I'm sorry. I'll turn it off."

"No, you don't have to..."

The screen went blank, and she turned to me. "Are you in some kind of trouble at school?"

"School's fine."

"Then, what is it? I'm not blind. I can see there's something wrong."

Should I tell her?

"Only thing is, I want to do something."

She reached across the table and put her hand on mine. "What? What do you want to do?"

"Something important, something that matters."

"But you matter to me. You're all I have."

At least tell her about the posters.

But I just fiddled with my last bite of chicken nuggets. "It's nothing. I'm just tired. I think I'll go to bed early."

She pulled her hand back. "Maybe that's a good idea. Go on to bed. I'll check in on you in a bit."

I went to my room feeling like a fool. I shouldn't have spoiled Mom's tv and I shouldn't have kept things from her.

Information in criminal investigations should be maintained on a need-to-know basis. -DENISON

The professor was right. Of course I shouldn't tell Mom. I should work out the details and go directly to the police; the FBI.

I got my pad.

1. Carl LePonte was in charge of Wraith's money. He disappeared in December just before millions of their dollars turned up missing.
2. Katz moved in last winter. Before or after December?
3. Katz's claim check was in the trasher bag with Wraith's money band
4. Katz doesn't handle his crutches well. Does he really need them?
5. Katz has a beard. Disguise?
6. Katz avoids everybody and doesn't seem to have any friends.

Katz had to be Carl LePonte, Wraith's missing money guy. But just to be sure, I still needed to check to see when he had moved in.

Mom rapped on the door and stuck her head in. "Sorry to bother you, honey, but your math teacher's on the phone."

Mr. Abramovitz calling here?

I hurried to the living room. Mom was just sitting down on the couch.

"Umm, Mom, could you hang this up? I think I'll use the phone in your room."

She stood and started down the hall. "That's alright. I'll go to the kitchen."

I waited until she got down the hall. "Hello."

"Hi, William, it's Charlie. Say, I found out from my friend at the Chicago Police Department that they're very interested in these case. They'd already heard about the call we made to the Des Plaines Police. How's that for action? Thing is, they need to maintain secrecy so they want all the evidence you have. They need the matchbook, the wrapper, the money band, everything. They feel they're close to catching our embezzler, you know, Chameleon."

"But I thought the hoods at Wraith never pressed charges."

He paused. "I wasn't supposed to tell anyone, but have you heard of the Organized Crime Division of the Chicago Police

Department?"

"No."

"Well, they deal with mobsters and terrorists like the goons at Wraith and they need an informer; someone who's been on the inside."

I checked to be sure Mom couldn't hear and lowered my voice. "You mean they want to get Chameleon to squeal on the guys at Wraith?"

"I _knew_ you'd understand. The cops figure if they can protect Chameleon from the hoods at Wraith, he'll give them incriminating evidence to use against them."

"He or she."

"Uh, yeah, right. At any rate, bring the evidence, all of it, tomorrow. Try to get here by seven thirty because the police are sending a car around in the morning to pick it up. I'll meet you in the math room."

I put the phone back on the hook and walked slowly to my room, picked up my pad, and added to the list.

7. Why would the police want all my clues, but not want to talk to me?

8. Why would they go to the school to pick up the evidence instead of coming here?

It didn't fit. It lacked precision.

CHAPTER THIRTEEN
FIELD TRIP

I got to school early the next morning and went to the media room. There was no one at the copy machine, so in a few seconds I had copies of all the trasher clues. I put them in my notebook, and went on up to the math room. Mr. Abramovitz was at his desk grading homework.

"Hi, William. Be with you in a minute."

I sat at a front row desk and organized my evidence. The cleaners had the original claim check, of course, but Andrea had the photocopy she'd made at the drugstore. Otherwise everything was there; match book, candy wrapper, money band, and paper bag.

I looked at the bag. The hole that was burned in it was as neat as if someone had done it on purpose. None of the other evidence was scorched anywhere. I held the bag to my nose.

"On the scent of a crime?" Mr. Abramovitz had finished his grading and was standing up behind his desk.

"I was trying to figure out what this mediciney smell is."

He came around his desk, looked at the bag, and sniffed it. "Menthol, it's menthol from this cigarette burn on the bottom of the bag. There must've been a cigarette in the bag at some point. Maybe our chameleon smokes menthol cigarettes."

Never seen Katz smoke.

"I didn't have a chance to tell you last night but I think I know who Chameleon is and I don't think he smokes."

He picked up my stack of clues. "You really think you have an idea who it is?" He went back to his desk, put the clues in his center drawer, locked it, and came back around. "Whom do you suspect?"

"Milt Katz, this guy in my building."

He straightened his glasses. "Katz? What makes you think he's Chameleon?"

I told him about Andrea and the cleaner's claim check. He nodded his head and seemed real interested.

"And the cleaners said the claim check belonged to this Katz fellow?"

"Uh-huh."

"But there are lots of people named Katz. How do you know the one in your building is the right one?"

"They said <u>Milt</u> Katz."

"I see, that is pretty conclusive." Mr. Abramovitz sat back down at his desk. He picked up a letter opener and twirled its needle sharp point on his desk blotter. "Well then, William, I suppose you'd better get to class."

Class?

"But what about Katz?"

"I'll tell the police. They may want to talk to you, but right now you'd better get to class."

"I'm not going to class today."

He didn't say anything, he just stared out the window and continued to twirl his letter opener, so I left and walked downstairs to the administrative office.

One of the secretaries was at the front counter. "Yes, young man, may I help you?"

"I have this doctor's note."

I handed it to her and she read it. "Fine. I'll mark you down as excused for today. Have lots of fun at the doctor's."

Outside the school, the other kids were arriving ready to learn, or sleep, whichever. Either way I wasn't going to be there and I wasn't going to be at the doctor's office either, though the note I had typed and signed Mom's name to said I was. Okay, it wasn't honest, but I needed time if I was going to make sure Katz was caught.

I knew I had a full day ahead of me but I wasn't quite mentally ready to start. My talk with Mr. Abramovitz had left me uneasy. There was something about the way he wanted to handle things that I didn't like. I couldn't just refuse to cooperate though, he'd think I didn't trust him. Of course, I didn't completely trust him, which was why I had copied the trasher clues.

The school's old photo copy machine made crummy copies, but it was still stuck on two so at least I had an extra set.

A copy for Andrea. For the team.

As I walked past the front of the school, I could feel the strap of my backpack cutting into my shoulder. I had a lot of traveling to do and I didn't need my backpack slowing me down. No one was watching so I slipped into the bushes that ran in front of the school and dropped the backpack behind them. No one could see it there, and it was waterproof so even if it rained my stuff would be okay.

I hurried back across the park to the apartments. It was eight fifteen. Mom would be at work by now, and the Vipers would never expect me to be around during the day. I'd be able to work without hassles.

I spread my notes on the coffee table, hunted up a phone number I'd written down the night before, and punched it in. A man answered.

"Park Manor Apartments. Superintendent speaking."

"Hi, Dave, this is William Williamson."

"Well, howdy, Will. How you been keepin'?"

"Fine. Listen, do you remember when you lost Mrs. Oberonsky's rent check and I found it for you?"

"Owe you big for that one. They'd of canned me for sure."

Informants are crucial to detective work. -DENISON

"Well, I need some information and was hoping you could help."

"Sure thing. Whadaya need to know?"

"I need to know when Milt Katz moved in."

"To the building?"

"Yeah, only I don't want anyone to know I asked. That's important, okay?"

"Don't suppose it matters to no one. Let's see here, Milt moved in February ten. I remember 'cause it wasn't quite a whole month, but he paid for the whole. Said he didn't have nowhere else and we was cheaper than a hotel."

"You sure of that date?"

"Yep, February ten."

I thanked him, hung up, made a few notes, and punched up another number.

One ring this time and a woman answered. "Chicago Police Department, Central Division."

"Hello," I tried to sound grown up, "may I have the organized crime division?"

"I'm sorry, sir. The department does not have an organized crime division, as such. If you would like the number of the FBI, I believe they have a listing for, yes, here it is, the Federal Organized Crime Strike Force."

Did Abramovitz get it wrong?

"Uh, okay. Could I have that number?"
"In Chicago the number is 555-0213."
"Thanks. Oh, you had a car that's supposed to come by and pick up some clues, uh, evidence. Would you please tell them I won't be available until tomorrow?"
"I'll transfer you to dispatch, sir."
The phone clicked a couple of times and a woman's voice came on. "Dispatch."
"You had a car that was supposed to come to Morrison Middle School to pick up some evidence. Would you please tell them to wait until tomorrow?"
"What's the name?"
"Abramovitz, Charlie Abramovitz."
The phone was silent a minute or two then the woman came back. "I have no such order, sir. Are you sure you wanted the Chicago Police Department?"
He *faked* it.
"Sir? Sir?"
I hung up.
Abramovitz's story was fake. I'd suspected it, which was why I had called, but suspecting it and knowing it were two different things.
He lied, and badly. He didn't even sound like he believed it.
Bring everything—Secret informer—Not supposed to tell..."
I'd shared all my information with him, but he had held out on me. Why was he lying? Did he not trust me because I was a kid? Or did he just want to be the big man and catch Chameleon himself?
Or is *he* Chameleon?
The Professor practically shouted in my head.
Circumstantial and physical evidence are basic to the selection of probable suspects. -DENISON
Abramovitz was up to something alright, but he was not Chameleon. There was zero evidence connecting him to the trasher. Whatever it was that he was up to he wouldn't know what I was up to. He was scratched from my list of friends.
I took a couple of deep breaths to calm myself and looked at the list of jobs I'd made the night before. Number two was to search Katz's trash for more evidence. Maybe I'd find a link to Abramovitz.
This all started in the trash, maybe it'll end there.

All the apartments in my building had the kitchen next to the back hall. Each kitchen had a small two-way trash cupboard. All we had to do was open the kitchen-side door and put our trash in. Once a week the janitor would walk through the building, open the hall-side door, and collect the trash.

I snuck down the back hall to Katz's apartment and opened his trash door. There were two plastic bags inside. I dragged both of them to my apartment, into the kitchen, and dumped the first one out.

Yuck, *bananas*.

I hadn't been too crazy about going through someone's trash anyway, and the disgusting smell of rotten bananas didn't help. But now the trash was all over the floor. Since I had to clean it up anyway I figured I might as well examine it as I went.

As messy as the job was, at least I knew it wasn't illegal. Professor Denison said trash was in the public domain or public something or other, and that anyone could claim it. But legal or not, I felt like a peeping Tom.

Trash sure tells a lot about a person.

Most of what it told me wasn't very useful. I learned Katz liked Mexican food and beer. He ate little kids' kind of cereal and used lemon-scented dish soap. Dumb useless stuff but private. It wasn't until I was nearly finished with the first bag that I found something interesting. There were several past-due and final notices from utilities and other companies all bundled together with a rubber band. If Katz had millions in cash he wasn't spreading it around.

The first bag was finished, wrapped up, and ready to go to the trash for good. I looked at the second bag and wondered what was trapped inside.

Probably, tuna fish.

I could've skipped it. The first bag hadn't been much help, but it had pointed out that Katz was slow in paying bills.

"Okay, I'll do you, too."

I dumped the second bag onto the floor.

More Mexican food: two frozen burrito packages, some Mexican tv dinner boxes and trays, and three empty refried beans cans. Six beer cans, more past due-bills, and an unopened letter. The return address was Mount Hope Hospital, New York City.

Should I open it?

It was first-class, and I knew it was illegal to open another person's first-class mail. But was it still a letter or was it trash? I looked around the kitchen like someone might be watching.

If he'd wanted it, he wouldn't have thrown it away.

I got a knife out of the silverware and slit the letter open. It was a bill. Mount Hope Hospital was trying to collect four thousand three hundred ninety-three dollars and three cents. I was amazed that anyone could owe so much to a hospital. I read the itemized part of the bill. It had information about the services Katz owed for and it showed how much his insurance had paid. I was even more amazed when I saw that the insurance had paid Mount Hope over one hundred and sixty-five <u>thousand</u> dollars.

The bill described a long list of surgeries, but the language was too technical. The list of service dates clearly showed that Katz had been a real sick man in Mount Hope from October of last year to February eighth of this year.

The newspaper story from the library had said the embezzlement from Wraith happened in November and December of last year. During that time, Katz had been flat on his back, hundreds of miles away.

Andrea's brilliant work with the laundry claim check. My deductions about Katz. I had been so sure he was Chameleon. Now I was sure of nothing.

No, that wasn't true. There was still one thing I was sure of. Abramovitz knew as much as I did, and that was way too much for a man who couldn't be trusted.

CHAPTER FOURTEEN
A SAVAGE TURN

I looked at Mr. Katz's trash spread out on the kitchen floor. I'd stuck my nose in his sad life and I felt ashamed. I'd been stalking the wrong guy because of one piece of evidence, the stupid cleaner's claim check.

But he acts like such a fake. Those crutches, the way he struggles. He doesn't seem like—Like what? Like a cripple?

I could just hear the fit I'd thrown at Andrea's when she'd thought Katz was harmless because he was disabled. I was worse. I'd wanted him to be guilty because of his disability. I'd wanted to prove a guy could be anything.

A crook. A private detective.

Professor Denison had warned me a hundred times, but I'd still let my personal feelings screw me up. Not only that, I'd counted too much on a single piece of evidence.

But it seemed so clear. Chris swore the claim check was in the bag with the other trasher stuff and he wouldn't lie. If it didn't match the other trasher clues, how had it gotten there?

Everything would have to be checked again.

I felt discouraged and depressed. The horrible smell of dead bananas didn't help. I hadn't eaten much breakfast and it was past lunch time, but defeat and the foul stench had spoiled my appetite. I'd skip lunch, maybe dinner, too.

Never eat Mexican again.

I swept up the last of the trash, snuck down the back hall and put both bags back in Mr. Katz's bin, no point in making the janitor suspicious, then went back to the apartment and flopped on the couch.

Detective. Ha. More like defective.

I was completely wrong about Mr. Katz and I'd let Abramovitz fool me so easily with his "calls to the police." I hadn't heard any of the other side of his phone calls, he could've been talking to anybody or nobody.

Looked right at me and lied through his teeth!

At least I knew he wanted the trasher stuff bad enough to lie. He wanted to have it all so he could—Could what? Blackmail Chameleon for some of the stolen millions?

Go face him. If he won't come clean, call the FBI.

I went back to school, in the side door, and checked the hall clock. In fifteen minutes, seventh hour would be over. I could get at him then. Until then I'd have to go back outside or I might get hassled for being out of class.

I figured I could get my backpack and hide in the bushes until the last bell, but when I went around the corner of the school I saw three police cars, lights flashing. I jumped back out of sight.

The note! They know about my phony doctor excuse!

But that's stupid. They wouldn't send cops for a fake note. Must've been an accident or something.

I really needed a hiding place now, and the bushes were about the only good one around. I peeked around the corner again. The old evergreens straggled across the front of the building in a ragged, but solid line. They were badly overgrown and a bush cave had formed underneath them. The cops were busy measuring and taking notes, if I crawled from bush to bush they'd never notice me.

I slipped around the corner and ducked under the first bush. The blue of my backpack was easy to see twenty-five or thirty feet away. I started to crawl toward it.

Ye-ow!

I jerked my hand back. There was a rust colored sticker jutting out of my palm. I pulled it out, but I could see the ground ahead was covered with them. I reached back, pulled off my shoes, and put one on each hand. My heavy right shoe made a bizarre mitten, but for the first time since I'd gotten it I was glad I had it.

The closer I got to my backpack the closer I got to the cops. I could hear them talking and if I held my head just right I could see them. They were talking to a woman in a suit. Her back was to me, but she still looked familiar. When she turned and pointed down the street, I could see it was Ms. Potter, the school principal.

I worked my way closer, went past my backpack, and crawled to within a few feet of the cop cars.

"I can't imagine why he'd even want to go across the street," Ms. Potter said. "There's nothing there but apartment buildings."

"Maybe he knew someone who lived over there," a policewoman said.

"I couldn't say," Ms. Potter said. "This is all so distressing, and I know the children will be upset. Mr. Abramovitz is a favorite of theirs."

Abramovitz? What's going on?

"If you're through with me," Ms. Potter said, "I'd better get together with the staff. We'll need to be ready to counsel the children. Such a shame, so senseless."

She went back inside of the school and the police went back to measuring. I got my bag, crawled back to the edge of the building, and put my shoes back on my feet. The final bell rang and I went back in the side door.

School should've been out, but the halls were still empty. I took a couple of steps in and could hear Ms. Potter on the PA.

"...sort of thing. We all wish the best for his family, and I'm sure he will be in our thoughts tonight. There will be a special meeting for concerned parents this evening at seven o'clock in the east art room. Please tell your parents that if they would like more information they may attend. School is dismissed."

The kids began to come out of their classrooms, but instead of running and yelling they were talking quietly among themselves. I could make out bits and pieces.

"I had him last year," one girl said.

Another group of kids passed by,"...just to run him down like that. It's just so..."

What's happening?

I looked for a familiar face and saw Steve, from art class. "Hey, Steve, I was absent today. What's going on?"

"Pretty heavy, dude. Old man Abramovitz got nailed by a car right in front of the school. Some babe creamed him. Didn't stop or nothin', just, pow! And took off."

Oh, my God.

"Is he—dead?"

"Punted him clear from the street to the sidewalk. There's blood all over."

I put my hand against the lockers to keep from falling.

"You alright? Was he a friend of yours or something?"

"Yeah, something."

"Wow. Sorry, dude, bummer."

It's started. The killing's started. Have to stop it before...

WWW: Shadow of the Chameleon

I walked down the hall in a dream, no, a movie. I was an actor in a movie, and I would go to the office where they'd be waiting. I'd tell them everything and they would not believe me.

The office was totally deranged. Phones were ringing, people were rushing around. No one paid any attention to me. I walked past the counter and down the hall to Ms. Potter's door. She was on the phone. She waved her hand to shoo me away, but I knew my part.

She put her hand over the phone. "Young man, you will have to wait outside. We have a situation here—"

"I know who did it."

She gave me the surprised look I knew she would. "I'm sorry," she said into the phone, "I'll have to call you back."

She hung up, eyes on me. "You can identify the woman who hit Mr. Abramovitz?"

"I know *who* it is."

"You are one of my students, aren't you?"

"William Williamson, seventh grade. Mr. Abramovitz knew too much. That's why he was hit."

Her right eyebrow arched. "Knew too much? What do you mean?"

"Millions of dollars were embezzled from this company, and we were solving the case. I have the evidence in my backpack."

"Let me see."

I pulled the photocopies out of my backpack and handed them to her.

"I really don't see what all of this means. How is this evidence of a crime?"

That's my cue.

"I have to tell the police."

"William, this isn't something you were just playing with is it? Something from Mr. Abramovitz's Mystery Club?"

"It was a game, but it isn't now. The killer is the one who embezzled the money."

"Killer?" She straightened in her chair. "Mr. Abramovitz isn't dead. Didn't you hear my announcement? He's in intensive care, but he's still alive."

"He isn't dead?"

"That was the hospital I was talking to when you came in. They are listing him as critical, which means he's very seriously injured, but he is definitely still alive."

"I thought he was dead. I thought he was..."

"I understand. But, as you can imagine I am really very busy. If you have some information about the hit-and-run driver, please let me have it."

Snap out of it, dude. Do it right. Remember...

Emotional detachment is the hallmark of the professional detective. -DENISON

"The one who hit Mr. Abramovitz could be a woman or a man, Ms. Potter. Whoever it is would wear a disguise to do something like this."

"A disguise. Uh-huh, well, sometimes, William," she'd switched to her pat-on-the-head voice, "sometimes when we receive a shock, like we have today, we have difficulty accepting—"

"Ms. Potter, I'm sorry, but you don't understand. All of this is real. These things are really happening and they'll get worse if you don't help. Whoever did this may know about me, about the kids who helped me. If you don't want another hit-and-run in front of your school you'd better call the police in here right now."

Now you did it.

She sat for a moment then reached across her desk and pushed her intercom button.

A voice came over the intercom. "Yes, Ms. Potter?"

"Mark, are those officers still outside?"

"Uh, yes, they are."

"Ask the Sergeant to step in here for a moment, will you? Something's come up."

CHAPTER FIFTEEN
THE UPPER HAND

Ms. Potter motioned for me to have a seat, but before I could sit there was a knock at the door.

"Come in," she said.

The door opened and a policeman leaned in. "You wanted to see me?"

"Yes, sergeant, come in. This is William Williamson, and he has some information he feels will help us find the hit-and-run driver. He's a student here, and one of Mr. Abramovitz's friends. Apparently they were working on a mystery in the school's Mystery Club, and they—Well, why don't you tell him, William?"

My mind was buzzing with so many thoughts that it froze. All I could do was stare.

Come on, dude. Don't blow it.

I shuddered and the words came out. "A game. It all started with a game. Some of my friends and I wanted to see if we could figure out who had thrown some trash away just by examining it. The trash was weird, though, because it had a money band in it. You know, one of those paper things banks bundle money with."

"Yes, go on."

"This was a big one, though. I mean, it was a two thousand dollar one. Ms. Potter has photocopies of it."

Ms. Potter handed the photocopies to him and he examined them. "Are these front and back views?"

"Yes, sir. The initials on the front were written in ink and the name written beside them is 'Wraith.' I wrote that there because that's what the tiny writing around the W says." I pointed at the rubber stamped W. "See, right there. I showed it to Mr. Abramovitz and we figured out it was probably the initials of two people who had counted the money. The newspaper said Wraith is owned by a bunch of gun runners and dope dealers and that somebody embezzled money from them. That's who I think ran Mr. Abramovitz down."

"Gun runners?" the cop said. "You think gun runners ran your Mystery Club teacher down because he was embezzling money?"

Dang, pay attention.

"Mr. Abramovitz wasn't embezzling, one of Wraith's employees was. We didn't know for sure who it was so we gave him or her the code name 'Chameleon.'"

His eyes narrowed. "Let me get this straight. You found this money band and decided someone had stolen the money that was in it?"

"Yes."

"How do you know there was money in it?"

I hadn't thought of that. "I, uh, I don't know. Why else would anyone have one?"

He pushed his cap back on his head. "Son, if I walk down the street to the Chicago Trust Company, or for that matter, if you do, they'll give you, free of charge, as many of these bands as you want."

He turned to Ms. Potter. "I know we all want to find the perpetrator, and we have some good leads. We have several eyewitnesses, a description of the vehicle, and a partial plate number."

He patted me on the head, turned, and headed for the door. "Hang on to this stuff—this evidence, son. If we can't locate the perp we may want to look at it again."

"Wait a minute. It was glued."

He turned back toward me. "What was glued?"

"The money band. Get it? The money band was glued together. All we need is a stack of twenty hundred-dollar bills, or just twenty, one dollar bills would work. If we wrap the money band around the stack we can see if the glued spot fits right."

He gave Ms. Potter a pained look.

"I think we've used enough of the policeman's time, William." She straightened my stack of copies and looked at the cop. "Let us know what you find out. I'll contact you if we come up with anything useful."

"Thank you, ma'am," he said and left.

Ms. Potter handed the copies back to me. "I think the sergeant's explanation was more than satisfactory, don't you? Let's let the police handle this and let's concentrate on our schoolwork. I'm sure Mr. Abramovitz would want us to."

Her expression softened. "I know he's your friend, William,

I appreciate you're worried about him. But in real life explanations are more—they're more ordinary than the sort of thing you're talking about. Now, I need to call several people and it's time you went home."

There was nothing I could do. I put my copies in my backpack and left. In the hall I tried to think of my next move. The FBI? No, if the police didn't believe me it was no use talking to the FBI. They'd just say it was a police matter. But one thing I could do was get the original evidence out of Mr. Abramovitz's drawer.

I went to the third floor and started down the hall. As I was going past the science room, Mr. Dirk saw me.

"Willie," he said, "I thought you were excused today."

Oh, great.

"Yeah, I was, but I, uh, I came to get my homework."

"Oh, well come in. I'll get it for you in a minute, just got to put these doodads out."

Rats.

I went in the science room, sat, and watched Dirk hook up his "doodads," his Bunsen burners. I'd read about Bunsen burners in the lab section of the science book. They ran on natural gas and were used in experiments that needed heat.

He was struggling with a tangle of a burner's rubber hose.

Read your doodad book, Dirk.

"We're going to use these tomorrow, so you'll need to read about them for your homework. We're going to heat glass tubes and watch them flop around. Here, I'll show you how they work."

This ought to be good.

He fumbled with the gas and struck a match.

"FOOMP!"

Flame shot halfway to the ceiling.

"Whoa!" He tried to shut it off. "Damn cheap junk!" The flame was burning steadily at about four feet, and Dirk tried frantically to adjust it.

Finally he gave up and shut it off. "This stuff is so old it'll be a miracle if we don't blow our butts off tomorrow." His hands were still shaking, but he managed to hook up the last two burners. Then he went to his desk, hunted around, and pulled out a copy of the day's assignment.

I looked at it to be sure it was the right one and was amazed to see it was.

"I guess you heard about Abramovitz," he said.

"Yeah."

"Makes you think, doesn't it? One minute we're up here doing some dumb experiment, and the next the intercom gives you the bad news. I just can't imagine why he would've been out of the building during class like that."

"No, me neither. Thanks for showing me about the Bunsen burners. I have to get the rest of my assignments so I'd better go to my other class rooms now."

"Say, I'm about through here, want a ride?"

With *klutz* man?

"Thanks, but I need to walk."

"No trouble, right on my way."

"Thanks, but my doctor said I should walk for exercise."

"Okay, then I guess I'll see you tomorrow, Willmeister. Don't forget your fireproof underwear."

I went down the hall to the math room. There was no one there. This was my chance to look in the desk drawer. I checked to see if Dirk or anyone else was looking then zipped in and pulled on the middle drawer.

I remembered that Mr. Abramovitz had locked it when he put the clues away, but it slid open now and it was empty. I looked in the other drawers. They were crammed full of files and folders. There was no way I could search them all.

Maybe he took the clues home.

I shut the drawer, left the math room, and hurried down the stairs. I needed to talk with someone who understood. I needed to talk to Andrea.

Please, God, let me get to Andrea's without any Vipers.

God must have been listening. I made it to Andrea's building. The snooty front-desk lady wasn't there.

I zipped up in the elevator and punched Andrea's bell several times.

She yanked the door open. "Alright, alright, what's the big— William! What's happened?"

"It's Mr. Abramovitz. He got run down right in front of the school."

"The guy from your school? Well, come in."

I followed her to the living room. She sat on the couch and patted the cushion beside her. "Here, have a seat. Tell me everything."

I sagged down into the couch. "He left the building during class and somebody dressed like a lady ran him down. He's in critical condition."

She put her hand on mine. "Wow. Did they catch the driver? Was it Milt Katz?"

"No, the driver got away. And we were all wrong about Katz. I checked, and he was in a New York hospital when the money was embezzled. No way he could be Chameleon."

"But the lady at the cleaners said—"

I shook my head. "Forget it. Milt Katz was in the hospital the whole time. Chameleon has to be someone else."

She pulled her hand off mine. "Are you sure? I mean, the money band was right there in the bag with his the claim check for his cleaning."

Gently.

"Yeah, I know. It was hard for me to believe too, but I saw his hospital bill. No way he could've been anywhere near Wraith when the money was stolen. The real Chameleon must've just picked up the claim check to be neat, you know, in the lobby or some place. You were the one who said Chameleon was careless and neat."

The wrinkles on her forehead began to fade as the truth sank in. "Okay, alright, let's say Katz isn't Chameleon. Mr. Abramovitz must know who the real Chameleon is or he wouldn't have been run down. We'll have to go to the cops and tell them what we know or we might be next."

She started to stand but I held her arm. "I told this police sergeant everything we know. He didn't believe me. He treated me like a baby."

She twisted her arm from my grip. "We can tell my dad. He'll believe me."

"Okay, we'll tell your dad, but let's get something to tell him, first."

"What do you mean?"

I picked the telephone up from the coffee table. "Let's get a list of everyone who moved in to my building after the money was embezzled from Wraith but before Chris found the money band in our trash."

I called my informant.

"Park Manor Apartments. Superintendent speaking."

"Hi, Dave, this is William Williamson again. Sorry to bother you, but I need some more information."

"Sure, Will. What can I do you for?"

"I need a list of the people who moved into the building after last November first."

"Let me get the receipt book." He was gone for a few minutes. "Looks like just two since November. Ms. Woo, from over to the grocery store, and Norma Owens. Ms. Woo's in nine-fourteen, and Ms. Owens is in the penthouse. She travels, sells something or other. Oh, and Milt."

"You're sure that's all?"

"That's all I got."

"Okay, Dave. Thanks a lot. I owe you one."

I hung up and looked at Andrea. "There are only two. The first is a lady named Norma Owens. I've seen her only a couple of times. She seems real secretive, you know, suspicious. Also, she lives in the penthouse. That has to cost a bundle plus it's real private, make a great hideout. The other is Ms. Woo, from the grocery store across the street from me. I've known her all my life. No way she could be Chameleon so..."

Precision, dude.

"So Norma Owens is our best suspect. She, *or he*, is probably Chameleon."

CHAPTER SIXTEEN
A COLD WIND

I stood staring out the window. Shadows were slipping across the city like the fingers of a black hand. From deep in the darkening glass a pair of eyes stared back at me. I jumped and almost knocked Andrea down.

"What's the big idea?" she said.

I couldn't tell her I'd been scared by my own reflection. "Uh, saw something; bats or something."

"Well, don't do that. Scare me to death."

I snuck another look at my reflection.

Like a ghost. Like *my* ghost.

Suddenly, there was nothing I wanted more than to get home. Norma Owens, Vipers, they didn't matter. I wanted to get home, and I didn't want to wait to talk to Andrea's dad, or anyone else.

I went to the couch and grabbed my jacket.

Andrea followed me and caught me by the wrist. "You aren't going to leave, are you?"

"I have to go to my place; see if Norma's car hit anything." I pulled my arm away and slipped my jacket on. "Give Chris a call. Let him know what's happening."

"But what if she sees you messing around her car? I think we should tell my dad what we know."

"We'll tell him, and don't worry about Norma. She wouldn't do anything in her own building."

She stamped her foot. "Don't tell me she wouldn't do anything. She ran down that Abramovitz guy in broad daylight."

I picked up the phone from the coffee table. "I know, but she wouldn't risk giving away her hideout." I punched Chris's number in.

An answering machine came on. "Hebert residue. Unless we owe you money, leave a massage at the tone."

Guy's a riot.

"Chris, this is William. I need to talk to you about the

chameleon I have in my biology class. You remember the one I called <u>Mr. Katz</u>? Well, we changed his name. Get it? New name. Don't leave your apartment. This is very important. I'm at Andrea's and I'll be right over."

"I'd better get going," I said.

Andrea followed me to the door. "Why don't you call your mom?"

"She's working late but I'll be okay. I'm getting good at dodging the Vipers. I guess I can dodge Norma, too."

She stepped between me and the door. "Then I'm going, too."

Stubborn little...

"Listen, Chris is my friend. Besides, I have to go home sometime."

She crossed her arms. "If you leave here alone, I'm calling my dad."

Stubborn and ruthless.

"Okay, you can come, but walk way ahead. Norma couldn't know about you, but if she saw you with me—"

"Why don't we just take a cab."

I flashed on my slow motion escape from Chockie in the city's slowest taxi. "Cabs are useless. We'd never get one at rush hour, anyway."

She followed me downstairs, grumbling all the way. By the time we reached the lobby, she was grumbled out.

"Okay," she said, "I'll go ahead, but if you get in any trouble—"

"I'll scream or wave or something. Now, get going."

She pushed through the front door, pulled the collar of her coat tighter, and started for Park Manor. I waited about half a minute then followed. I had to pull my coat tighter, too. The temp had definitely dropped.

The taxi herd puffed along in clouds of steamy exhaust, all bunched together like they were trying to keep warm. An icy blast of wind cut the corner ahead of me and smacked me in the face.

Four blocks to go.

The traffic around me blurred through my cold-weather tears. I couldn't tell if the drivers were men or women, but I figured I'd be okay so long as I watched the street crossings. People might race around the city on tv cop shows, but no one could really do that in Chicago rush-hour. Moving was hard enough. Norma had taken a chance running Mr. Abramovitz down, but she'd have to be a fool to try it at rush hour.

And she's no fool.

The people on the sidewalk scurried by, wrapped in their thin fall coats, rushing to get out of the season's first blast of cold north wind. I caught a glimpse of Andrea through the shifting crowd. She was further ahead than I wanted her to be. I pulled my jacket tighter and picked up my pace. An opening appeared in the crowd, and I was just about to shoot through when a bandaged hand slammed down on my shoulder.

I spun around. Even through his mummy bandages I knew Chockie Bortka's face.

Run!

I darted away, bumping into people, signs, parked cars.

Get away!

I dumped my backpack on the sidewalk, sprinted as hard as I could.

From behind came Chockie's voice. "Hey, kid! Hold it!"

I raced around a corner where the darkness had thickened. Chockie was right behind me. Traffic noise, windows, faces, all swirled together. I had to run, get away. Pain didn't matter. Fear, just fear.

Then tumbling down into parked cars and darkness.

Lights flashing. I looked up from the floor of a cold dark forest. Red lights flashing. Trees towering above, swaying.

Clearer now. Faces out of the swirling light.

Get up! Run!

But I was pinned to the ground.

"Take it easy, Bill, you're hurt, bad." It was like a voice from another room; from a dream.

I closed my eyes, said a jumbled prayer, then opened.

Chockie!

"Take it easy, take it easy." His big hand was pressing against my chest. "Didn't mean to scare you, Bill. Just wanted to thank you for gettin' that dog off me."

What?

"Alright, back off everybody." A man in a uniform pushed through the crowd and he bent down beside me. "Fire-rescue, son. Just lie still. We're going to take you for a little ride to the hospital. We'll call your folks as soon as we get there. Do you live around here?"

"Yes."

"Just relax. We're just going to take a short ride in the ambulance."

"Don't worry, Bill," Chockie said, "I got your stuff. I'll follow 'em to the hospital. Don't worry, you're gonna be okay."

The crew lifted me onto a stretcher and slid me into the back of the ambulance. The doors bumped shut and the siren came on.

The last time I'd ridden through town on my back was when I was a little boy, lying with my head in Mom's lap. I watched the red flashing lights reflect off the buildings we passed. I wasn't worried. My leg didn't hurt. I couldn't even feel it. I wasn't even sure if I was dreaming...

New face, now. "William? William, can you hear me?" It was Dr. Grinter, my foot specialist.

"Hi, Doctor."

"Listen, William, you're at the hospital. You've had a little accident. You've hurt your leg and bumped your head." He shined a light in one eye then the other. "I want to take a closer look at your leg and I'm going to give you an anesthetic. Do you understand?"

"Okay."

He turned to someone behind him. "Have you contacted the home?"

"Dad's dead," I said.

"I know. It's alright. Your mom will be here soon. Are you in any pain?"

"Head hurts."

"How about your leg?"

"No."

He was working on my right, my bad leg. "Can you feel this?"

"No."

"How about this?"

"Think so."

"Good. We'll have you fixed up in no time."

The lights dimmed...

"Billy?" It was Mom. "Billy, can you hear me?"

I opened my eyes.

"Billy, Dr. Grinter is here. They need to give you an anesthetic. Understand?"

I nodded and the dark came back.

As soon as I woke, I knew where I was. I'd been in a hospital bed before. The ambulance, Dr. Grinter, it all came back. I looked down at my leg. It was in a long cast and the cast was hung from a frame by wires. I was used to that, too. I'd had six operations on my leg. This was seven.

Damned leg.

Mom was asleep in the chair by the bed.

"Mom, what time is it?"

She woke up, came over, and took my hand. "It's..." she looked at her watch, "it's seven-thirty."

I looked around the room. "What day?"

"Thursday morning. You've been asleep for almost thirteen hours. How you feeling?"

"Fine."

"Does your leg hurt?"

"Huh-uh."

"I'm sorry you had to come back, sweetie. I know it's hard in the hospital, but, Dr. Grinter says you can probably go home in about a week if you do well." She patted my hand. "Andrea said to say hello so did Chris."

"Where are they?"

"Probably getting ready for school, but Andrea said not to worry, that she'd taken care of everything. She said wanted me to tell you that she, uh, lets see now. She said she walked right by a lizard and it didn't even look at her. Whatever that means."

"Lizard or chameleon?"

"That's right, chameleon. What are you kids up to anyway?"

"Just a game. Not important."

"Well, she thought it was. She made me promise I'd tell you and she looked so serious."

"That's just Andrea."

She'll tell her dad. The cops'll believe him.

Mom fluffed up my pillow being careful not to move me. "Do you think you could eat a bite?"

"I guess so."

"Would you like a little gelatin?"

"Anything but Mexican."

She put her hand to my forehead.

"Just a joke, Mom. I'm alright."

Mom buzzed for the nurse, and a few minutes later she came bustling in. "How are we feeling this fine morning? Are we ready for some breakfast?"

"Yes, please. Could I have some cereal?"

"Just mark down what you want and I'll have it sent up."

I looked at the list she gave me and put a check by Wheaties and white toast.

"I have your medication," she said. "Do you think you can take it lying down or do you want me to lift your head?"

"I can take it." I took the pill from her, swallowed it, and put my head back on the pillow. I knew the routine. I was to lie still like a helplessness little baby. And just when I'd been so close.

Damned leg.

Tears pooled up in my eyes. I turned my face to the wall.

Mom patted my hand again. "Don't worry, the doctor says you've made such progress over the last year that this operation might even make you stronger."

She doesn't get it. Can't be a detective if I can't even run a couple of blocks.

"It's alright, sweetie," she said. "Go ahead and have a good cry. But it's going to be alright, you'll see."

Mom cried too, and I felt better. Her hand was on mine, and it all made me feel better. She was right, I'd do something else. I could be a mathematician like—

Abramovitz...

I pulled out a corner of pillowcase and used it to wipe my eyes. "You're right, Mom. It's going to be okay."

She wiped the tears from her face and smiled. "You're a good boy, Billy. I'm glad you're mine."

"I'm glad, too. Anyway, could've been worse. My math teacher, Mr. Abramovitz, was hit by a car. He may be right here at the hospital."

"Your math teacher? When did this happen?"

"Yesterday, same as me."

"What a shame. But it doesn't surprise me. The way some people drive, you'd think they were trying to hit you."

Got that right.

"If he is here, can I go see him?"

"Not for awhile."

I looked up at the wires holding my leg up and holding me prisoner. I wanted to rip them out. I took a deep breath.

Patience, patience.

But if Norma Owens thought I was a threat, patience wouldn't help. I looked through the open door of my room into the hall. Women walked by dressed in hospital white; the color

of friend and healer, but...
  Chameleon can turn white, too.

CHAPTER SEVENTEEN
HAUNTED

The bright lights in the hospital's hall had shone down on a crowd of people all day. Now it was the middle of the night, and their cold glow lit only empty halls.

My room was dark and gloomy. The only light was a shaft slanting in through the door. Mom stirred in her chair, got up, and came to my bedside.

"Want anything, honey?" she whispered.

I gazed up through hot watery eyes, but I was too weak to speak.

She stroked my head and kept watch. For a long time she stood, her hand on my arm. Then she gently slipped away.

"*Come with me.*"

The voice came from the shadows by the door. A horrible ice water feeling surged through me. I stared into the darkness, but there was nothing there.

"*You can't stay. There's no hope, no hope.*"

I wanted to answer the lifeless voice, to say something, anything, but I couldn't speak, and when I tried I couldn't move.

A wild-looking bearded man appeared out of the shadows wheeling a wheel chair. He came noiselessly toward the bed, closer and closer until his face was next to mine, his stale breath on my cheek.

Katz!

It was Milt Katz, but something was horribly wrong.

There were wires coming from his shoulders. There were wires in his head and coming from his jaw; all strung to an invisible place on the ceiling.

His jaw moved like a puppet's. "*I knew it was you.*" He reached a withered hand toward me. "*Come with me. There's no hope, no hope.*"

I woke with a violent gasp. "Don't let it take me!"

"Hush, hush now." Mom was beside me, stroking my hair. "Shhh, hush. It was just a bad dream, honey. No one's going to take you anywhere."

My breath was coming in gasps. I looked frantically around the room.

"There's no one here." She reached across me and turned my reading light on. "See? No one."

She got a damp cloth and wiped my face. "Are you alright now?"

The cloth had helped, but I was still looking around the room.

"Here," she said, "I'll turn on the other light."

She went to the door and flipped the switch to the overhead florescents. The bright light burned my eyes. I blinked then looked carefully around the room. The phantom was gone. I looked down the bed to the heavy cast on my leg. I traced the wires holding it up and shuddered.

It had breathed on my face only moments before, but the light had chased it away; the light and Mom. She moved her chair up close to the bed and she left the light on for the rest of the night. That kept the ghost away. It also kept us awake.

For hours I lay motionless in the bright light thinking of Mr. Katz, of frozen dinners and a sad, sour, solitary life. I thought back to my other stays in the hospital, of hospitals yet to come, and of hopelessness and defeat.

Outside, the people of the city would soon get up and go about their business, but I would stay here or in some other hospital.

The case. Chameleon...

Andrea would have to deal with that. Andrea, and the others. I could do nothing. I was helpless to stop Norma Owens. She would keep her millions and she would mess with anyone she wanted to. Or she would be caught. It didn't matter anymore, it wasn't up to me.

Useless, helpless, useless.

I watched the walls slowly lighten as the sun crept up. The new day had arrived, but not for me.

"Anybody home?" The day nurse was leaning in the door. "I have a surprise for you. Feel up to a surprise?"

Mom got up from her chair. "What sort of surprise?"

The nurse came in carrying a huge bouquet and a couple of brightly wrapped packages.

"Some of your little friends were here very early to see you, but the doctor still has you marked for no visitors so they left these with me."

The sight of the flowers instantly cut through my depression. I carefully shifted myself on the bed and held out a hand for the presents.

"There are lots of other things at the nurses' station," she said, "I'll go get them."

Mom was busy arranging flowers. "Isn't that nice of your friends to come all the way over here on a school day? Who are the presents from?"

I turned the packages around and read the tags. "This one's from Chris and this one's from the kids in my art class. But today isn't a school day, it's all-district conference. If I weren't in here, I'd have the day off."

"Oh, that's right," Mom said. "Did you want me to speak with your teachers?"

Before I could answer, the nurse bumped through the door with a cart full of flowers and packages. She and Mom started unloading.

"We had a tv actor in here last month," the nurse said. "Even he didn't get this much stuff."

"William has wonderful friends," Mom said.

I looked at the mountain of stuff. When I was in the hospital before, I hadn't gotten half so many goodies.

Some things *are* improving.

I felt almost as if I was surrounded by my buds. Presents from the school, Chris, and Andrea. For the second time since I wound up in the hospital, I cried.

I'd felt so alone in the night. I'd given up on me, and in a way, I'd given up on my friends. I probably didn't deserve such loyal friends but I sure was glad I had them.

"What would you like for breakfast?" the nurse asked. "Your orders say you can have anything you want."

"Could I get some scrambled eggs and bacon? Maybe some toast and jelly?"

"Sure, and I'll see if I can find something for your mom. By the way, your friends said they would be back later this morning. I told them to call first, but I imagine you'll be able to have visitors by then."

I was even happier about the idea of visitors. I hoped both Andrea and Chris could come. The old feeling was back just as if it had never left. I was dying to know what was happening with the case and to know if they were safe. I asked the nurse for a pencil and pad and began to make some notes. There were some questions I wanted to ask Andrea and I wanted to stay organized.

Breakfast came for Mom and me and it was pretty good. Not as good as Mom's cooking, but pretty good. I was so hungry that after I ate my toast and jelly I licked out my plastic jelly thing.

Since I wasn't going anywhere, I decided to watch tv. I was in the middle of a cartoon featuring flying rabbits when Chris poked his head into the room.

"They said we could visit if you felt okay. Do you feel okay?"

"Sure, come on in."

Chris came in, followed by Andrea. Andrea stopped in the middle of my flowers and plants. "Wow, where'd you get all these flowers? There must be fifty things."

Chris held up a vase of yellow mums. "These are the ones I sent. Wait till you see the present I got you. Can I sign your cast?"

"Okay, but no pictures. The last time everybody thought I had a spider on my cast."

"I can draw better now. Can't I do a fighter plane?"

"Name, only."

Chris asked Mom for a pen, but all she had was a pencil. She went to the nurses' station to get a pen.

As soon as she left, I started to quiz Andrea. "What's going on? Did you tell your dad?"

Andrea checked to be sure no one was listening at the door then leaned over to me. "Norma moved."

"Moved out?"

"In the middle of the night. Your talky building superintendent said she put the keys in an envelope and shoved it under his door sometime Wednesday night."

"Right after Mr. Abramovitz was run down," I said.

Chris squeezed up close to Andrea and whispered. "She's the bad guy."

"She's the one alright," Andrea said, "Your super said she was paid up for the rest of the year. So she's rich enough to walk out on a penthouse apartment with over two months paid up on the lease.

"You sure were right about how your super likes to talk. Did you know, for instance, the elevator to the penthouse has a key?"

"Yeah."

"Well, he said that a couple of times he saw a man kind of sneak in and use a key to go up by himself."

Good old Dave.

"Did he know the guy?"

"He never got a real good look at him, but he said he always had a lumpy bag, like a bookbag."

"Like a school bookbag?"

"Yeah. Like a teacher might have."

I could tell she was waiting for me to say it: "So it could have been Abramovitz."

She smiled. "The school is right across the park."

"Excellent. Did you tell your dad?"

She reached into her coat pocket. "You haven't even seen the best thing yet. I have a picture."

She handed it to me. It was a kind of blurry shot of a big living room. In the corner was Norma Owens reading some piece of paper.

"Where in the world did you get this?" I asked.

"From your super. He took it the day Norma moved in. Seems he always gets pictures so he can prove what the apartment looked like in case someone trashes it. It isn't very good, though."

I handed it back to her. "It's good enough, the police can blow it up. You've got to have your dad take it to them right away. They have some eyewitnesses to the hit-and-run. One of them might be able to ID her."

"Yeah, probably," she said, "but if I went to Morrison I might be able to find witnesses, myself."

"*No way.* We've gotta get this to the cops, right away. Maybe we'd better just have my mom take it over."

She looked at me like I was crazy. "You want to ask your mom, the woman who hates all cops, to take something to the police?"

"Okay, not mom. But you'd better give it to your dad, or someone."

Mom came back into the room with Chris' pen, we dummied up.

"Thanks, Mrs. Williamson," he said and bent over my cast to do his thing.

He scribbled for a while then looked back at Mom. "This pen doesn't work too good. Can we see if they have a better one?"

Chris gave Andrea what he thought was a secret wink, but

I saw it. He and Mom went back to the hall in search of another pen. Andrea waited until they were out the door then turned back to me.

"Before they come back," she said, "I want you to open my present. It's a special."

That what we'd always said when we were little: "It's a special."

She handed me a small flat package tied with a pink bow. "What is it?"

She slipped her hand into mine. "Something to remind you you're not alone."

The warmth of her hand and the soft smell of roses. Then she was above me. Then she was kissing me.

Tingles to the toes.

She pulled slightly back and looked at me with her hazel-green eyes. I put my hand on the back of her neck and pulled her to me.

Excellent.

The door whooshed open and the day nurse came in. Andrea straightened up, blushing.

"I'm afraid we are going to have to break you two lovebirds up, for now. The doctor's due any second and he's easily embarrassed."

I squeezed Andrea's hand and whispered. "Be careful. Don't take any chances. Take the picture and the rest of our stuff to your dad."

Her hand tensed. "I've done it right so far haven't I?"

"Sure, but..."

"Well, then don't be bossy and don't worry."

But I was worried.

Mom came back in. "What's the matter, Billy?"

"You asked me a bazillion times already. There's nothing wrong."

She looked like her feelings were hurt so I softened my voice. "I guess these guys have to go. Are you going to come back tomorrow?"

Chris fished around in his pocket. "Sure, we'll be back. Here, I got you a candy bar."

"Thanks."

He handed me a Toblerone. It had the exact same wrapper as the one from the trasher.

I winked at him. "Thanks."

"You're welcome."

"I'll be careful where I throw the wrapper," I said and we all laughed. Mom laughed too. She didn't get it but she laughed.

"I need to get a few things," she said, "so I think I'll drive Chris home. Andrea's mom is downstairs waiting for her. I'll be back this afternoon."

They filed out the door. Andrea was the last to leave. She smiled her sweet smile then she was gone.

First time. Most excellent.

I picked Andrea's present and peeled the paper off carefully. Inside was a framed shadow-silhouette of a little girl. Across the bottom was written, "Andrea Braintree, Kindergarten-A, Parker Elementary School." I turned it over. On the back she had written, "WW, my love forever, Little Shadow."

The room door banged open and startled me so badly I almost dropped Andrea's picture. Dr. Grinter came in and stopped a couple of steps inside the door.

"Where'd you get all these flowers, William?"

"From friends."

"Sure have a lot of friends."

He made his way through the flowers to the foot of my bed and picked up my chart. "We got the postoperative x-rays back, and I think we've managed to improve the structure of your foot in a couple of pretty significant ways. I don't want to get your hopes up too high, but I think once the cast is removed you'll be able to get around better."

"Will I still need the shoe?"

"That's kind of up to you. If you're a good patient, like you always have been, then we may be able to put you in a more standard shoe with inserts." He paused. "On the other hand, if you don't keep still..."

"I know, you don't have to say it."

He took a long look at me like he was guessing my weight. "I'm going to break a rule. If you'll promise to restrict your activities to riding in a wheel chair, I'll remove your wires."

"Today?"

"Unless you had other plans."

"No, I mean, yeah, sure, I promise."

He went into the hall and returned a few minutes later with an orderly and a wheelchair. The orderly helped him remove the wires from my cast. It felt great not having my foot higher than my head. My butt had gone totally to sleep.

Dr. Grinter collected the last of the wires and wound them around his hand. "First rule is the last rule. Go easy."

I smiled at him and he left.

The orderly cleared a path through my flowers and helped me into the wheelchair. Moving was a little painful, but I expected that. I propped my right leg up with the chair's support and sat with my cast pointed at the door.

"Where to?" the orderly asked.

"I have a friend I think is here in the hospital. He was in a car accident. Could you check and see if he's here?"

"Is he a kid?"

"No, an adult. One of my teachers."

The orderly went to the door. "What's his name?"

"Charlie Abramovitz."

"Wait here. I'll see if I can find his room number."

He left and I was alone in the middle of my collection of plants and presents. One of the presents was a stack of video games held together with duct-tape. There was a note on top.

"Im sory you was hurt and Im sory I scared you Im your freind and I will take care of you personly. And thees games arnt stole. I pade for them. your bud Chockie."

Chockie? For a *friend*? This would take some getting used to.

The orderly came back looking worried. "How much do you know about this Abramovitz guy?"

"Is he dead?"

"No, but pretty banged up. He's listed as family only for visitors. You aren't family, are you?"

"I'm a real good friend."

"Well, I'll take you by and we can see if he wants any visitors."

He pushed me to the elevator and after some maneuvering fit me in. We went down three levels to the fourth floor. I was glad the elevator was slow. My leg was starting to throb and ache, and I didn't want any jiggling.

Mr. Abramovitz was in the room right next to the intensive care unit. His bedside light was on, but he looked like he was asleep. Both his legs were in casts, and the casts were hanging from a frame just like mine had been. One arm was propped to his side in a cast that looked like an airplane wing.

The orderly left me parked by Mr. Abramovitz's door and

went to the nurses' station to check in. On the wall by the door was a sign that read, "Family Only. Please Keep Visits Brief." I wheeled myself into the room.

"Mr. Abramovitz," I said as I neared the bed, "it's William." Nothing.

"Mr. Abram—Charlie. It's me, it's William."

He stirred slightly, half opened one eye, and looked at me for several seconds.

The orderly came back. "The nurses said no," he whispered.

"Just a second," I said. "It's real important. It might help catch the lady who hit him."

The orderly was behind me with his hands on the chair. He didn't pull or push so I figured I had my minute.

"Charlie, I know who hit you. It was Norma Owens, from my apartment building. Do you think you could identify her if I showed you a picture?"

He opened his other eye and moved his lips.

"I can't hear him," I said. "Can you get over by him?"

The orderly came around to the bed and leaned over. Charlie seemed to be saying something, then his eyes closed again.

The orderly came back around behind me and turned my chair toward the hall.

As soon as we were out of the room, I motioned for him to stop. "Did he say anything?"

"Plain as day, he said, `Chameleon, two copies.'"

CHAPTER EIGHTEEN
HOT PURSUIT

The orderly wheeled me into the elevator and we started back up to my floor.

Two copies? What sis he mean by, "Chameleon, two copies?"

The orderly had appeared at the side of my chair. "...huh, kid?"

"What?"

He squatted down even with me. "I said, do you know what he meant by that chameleon thing?"

"No, he must have been delirious. They get that way sometimes don't they?"

"Too bad. He looked like he knew you. The nurse said he didn't even recognize his own mother this morning. Oh yeah, she also said the police were sending a guard over. Your friend must've got in trouble over the accident."

"Something like that."

He wheeled me to the sun deck which was this big open room with a view of the lake front. I told him I wanted to stay there for a while and he said I should just tell the nurse when I wanted to go back to my room.

I sat and watched the distant waves and thought about Charlie.

Why would the police suddenly want to send a guard to protect him? Or was the orderly right, was Charlie in trouble? Whatever it was, I'd have to leave Andrea to deal with the police; she had the picture.

A pretty lady nurse got up from the desk by the door and came over. "Would you like something to read?"

"Could I have some paper and a pencil?"

"Certainly, just a moment."

She went to her desk and got me the paper and a pencil. I thanked her and started making some notes.

Two copies, two copies of Chameleon? Could be two

people involved. Copies could mean fakes, imitations. It could be two copies, or too copies, or two copy's, or to copy's. Could be Chameleon had two copies of something, or someone, or—

Photocopies!

The school machine always makes *two copies*, but Charlie picked only one up. He left a copy in the machine!

The pencil fell from my hand, rolled across the floor, and came to rest against a potted plant. One of the patients picked it up and brought it back to me.

"Are you okay?" he asked. "You need the nurse?"

I stared blankly past him. "Photocopies."

"I think there's a machine in the gift shop." he said.

"What?" I looked at him like he'd dropped from the sky.

"A photocopy machine. I think there's one in the gift shop."

"Oh, sure. Thanks."

Gotta get a hold of Andrea.

I pulled and pushed on the wheels of my chair. The nurse came over. "Would you like to move to a new spot?"

"I have to get to my room. Please hurry!"

She wheeled me back to my room.

"Do you want me to help you back into bed?" she asked.

"Just leave me alone."

She looked peeved, but she left. I grabbed the phone and called Andrea. Her mom answered.

"This is William, William Williamson. Is Andrea there?"

"Well, hello William. No, she isn't. She went over to Morrison. She said she wanted to get your assignments for you."

"Morrison! How long ago did she leave?"

"Just after we got back from visiting you. Must have been ten minutes or so."

"Listen, Ms. Braintree, Andrea's in real trouble. You have got to get over to Morrison and pick her up."

"What trouble? What is it?"

"No time to explain, just get over there and find her!" I hung up.

Did she believe me? Who will believe me?

I closed my eyes and said a quick prayer. The door to my room swung open.

"Okay if I come in?"

There in the doorway stood an angel disguised as Chockie

Bortka. He had a new leather jacket, his bandages were gone, and although his stitches still showed, the big jerk looked great.

"Chockie, man am I glad to see you."

"You are?"

"I'm in big trouble, you've gotta help me."

His chest swelled. "Just say it, Chockie'll do it."

"I have a friend who's in a jam over at Morrison. Can't call the cops, too slow. You've got to get me there right now."

"In your jammies? It's kinda cold, dude."

"Oh, yeah. I'd never get out of here dressed like this anyway. Maybe my clothes are in the closet."

Chockie looked in the closet and found my shirt, jacket, and shoes. My pants were missing.

"They probably cut them off me after the accident."

"No sweat, bud. Get in your shirt and stuff, I'll be right back."

Chockie ducked out the door. In a couple of minutes he was back with a white pair of pants. He tossed them to me.

"Where'd you get these?"

"A guy down the hall gave 'em to me."

"What guy?"

"The guy without no pants."

I braced myself for the pain and Chockie and I pulled the pants over my cast. I'd apologize to their owner later.

"Get me to your car," I said, "we've got to get to Morrison as fast as we can."

"Okay, man, but are you sure it's cool? I mean, what about your leg?"

Dr. Grinter's warning echoed in my ears.

"Leg's okay. Let's go."

Chockie grabbed the back of my chair and the two of us shot down the hall at breakneck speed. He took me down to the emergency entrance on the ground floor and parked me by the door.

"Wait here," he said, "I gotta get the wheels."

I waited and fretted. How could I have been so stupid? Of course Chameleon had to be someone at the school, someone who knew we were on to them. How else would they have discovered what Charlie knew. The photocopy machine that always made two copies had spilled the beans. Charlie had left a second copy of the money band in the machine and someone had found it. Someone in the teacher's lounge or the media room.

Who had been there?

I thought back. There was something about that day, something unpleasant.

"Pajama top!" I said. A lady in a flowered dress looked at me funny.

I remembered now how rude Dirk had been at the copy machine, how he'd said Mr. Abramovitz's shirt looked like a pajama top. Hadn't he also said something about making copies?

Dirk was a weak useless teacher. He couldn't even remember our names—Except on Wednesday, he'd remembered my name Wednesday. He'd been interested and nice, even offered me a ride home. Glad to do it, he'd said. On his way, he'd said, *but how did he know where I lived.*

An ambulance roared up to the emergency entrance and screeched to a halt. The driver hopped out and dashed across the drive toward me.

Chockie!

"Come on, bud," he said, "I hopped us some *good* wheels."

He didn't wait for objections. He wheeled me out to the ambulance, popped the rear door, and with a single swift motion lifted me and the chair into the back compartment. "No time to tie you down. Hang on."

He slammed the rear door. I grabbed the side railing with one hand and locked the chair's wheel lever with the other and we exploded out of the driveway, tires smoking, siren wailing.

My only view of things was through the rear window, and from what I could see of the horrified drivers we passed, I was glad I couldn't see out the front. The big ambulance swerved, screamed, and roared like a race car. Up on sidewalks we went, broad-sliding around corners. Trucks, cars, pedestrians, small animals scrambled to get out of the way.

Chockie knew the streets and wasn't picky about one-way signs so in just minutes we were screeching to a halt in front of the school. He jumped out, ran to the back, opened the door, and lifted the chair and me out.

"This the place?"

I was woozy from the roller coaster ride. "Yeah, third floor."

Chockie bent over and lifted me from the chair. "Hang on my neck."

Pain shot up my leg. The world whirled around. For a second I couldn't breathe. Chockie held on to me with one huge arm, reached down with the other, and picked up the wheelchair. Carrying us both, he bounded up the front steps two at a time. He jerked the heavy door open, slammed the wheelchair down, put me in it, and we zoomed down the main hall.

We reached the stairs to the upper floors. He hoisted me and the chair again. "Hang on, Bill, gonna run."

I clenched my teeth and held on as tight as I could and Chockie charged up the three flights of steps. At the top he put me back in the chair, and we shot down the hall to Dirk's room.

No one there.

One of the eighth grade teachers had followed us into the science room. "And just what do you young men think you're doing?"

"Looking for this girl," I said. "She was just here with a picture of a lady. Did she talk to you?"

"She came by my room a few minutes ago, but I don't see—"

"Did she come down this way?"

"I'm sure I don't know, but you young men can't just come whooping in here like savages. This is a *school* building. I'd better have your names."

Chockie picked up a stool in one hand.

"No, Chockie," I said, and he eased it down.

"Was that supposed to be a threat?" the teacher said. "Because if it was—"

"It wasn't," I said. "He just gets excited. Now please, I've just come from the hospital. My leg is killing me. I wouldn't have come if it wasn't an emergency. *I need to know where Mr. Dirk is.*"

"Are you scheduled to see him?"

"Yes, alright. I have him for science. My name is William W. Williamson and I need to see him right now!"

"It isn't necessary to raise your voice. I'm sure he's here somewhere. I saw him getting out of a little red sporty car when I came through the parking lot this morning."

The teacher went to the window. "It's still there. No, wait, it just started up."

"Chockie, check it out."

Chockie vaulted over a couple of rows of desks and looked out the window. "Only car moving's a red Porsche."

"That's the one," the teacher said.

"You've got to stop him," I said. "Hurry! He's a kidnapper."

Chockie bulldozed his way back through the desks and ran for the stairs, the teacher trailing in his dust.

I tried to get to the windows, but the room was full of Chockie's overturned desks. I only managed to get my chair and cast tangled up.

I could hear shouting and the squeal of tires. I tried to stand, but my cast was too bulky and my leg hurt too much. I'd have to wait.

I sat, straining to hear what was going on downstairs. I could hear something, but I wasn't sure what it was. I held absolutely still.

There was a muffled cry but it wasn't coming from the parking lot. It was coming from the equipment closet in the front corner of the room.

"Who's there?"

I could hear the sound of a struggle coming from inside the closet. The door popped open and Dirk stood up holding Andrea with a hand over her mouth and her arms pinned behind her back.

"Hello, Willie boy. Come to save your girlfriend? Isn't that sweet. The little cripple wants to be a hero."

"Let her go."

He dropped his phony smile. "I'm afraid I can't do that, Willie. You kids have caused a big problem for me and now I'm going to need your sweetie to help me get out of here."

He dragged Andrea to the window and looked out onto the parking lot. "Norma, you witch. Running out on me in my own car."

"She won't get far," I said.

"No? Well, neither will you, Willie boy."

Dirk released Andrea, reached into his pocket, and pulled out a small pistol.

My chair was next to a lab table. From where Dirk stood, he couldn't see me slip my hand across the table top and put it on the valve for the gas jet. "You wouldn't shoot a kid in a wheelchair would you?"

"You make it sound worse than it is, Willie."

I slowly twisted the valve open, picked up a book of matches that was on the table, and slipped my hand back across the table.

"Matches from The Central Bank of Chicago." I said. "Just

like the ones we found in Norma's trash. It was her tidy habits that led us to you."

"I'm pretty tidy too." He raised the gun toward me. "I always clean up my messes."

"Andrea, duck!"

With one motion I struck a match, tossed it at the gas jet, and ducked below the desk top.

"WHAM!"

The gas cloud exploded, knocking Dirk to the floor. The fire alarm clanged and the sprinklers erupted.

Dirk was lying semi-conscious on the floor. I gripped the wet wheels of my chair and with all my strength pushed my way through the overturned desks and crushed his gun hand with the wheel of my chair. He dropped the gun and rolled over screaming in agony.

"Run, Andrea!" But she kicked the gun under a lab table, grabbed my chair, and pulled me out of the room.

We got to the hall and Chockie was charging up the stairs.

"The guy on the floor," I said, "he's got a gun."

Chockie frowned. "Chockie don't like guns."

With his big fists clenched he went into the room. There were brief sounds of a scuffle, and a moment later he came out pulling an unconscious and drenched Dirk by one foot.

"Sorry, Bill," he said, "dude slipped."

FINALE
AT THE HOSPITAL

It had been a couple of weeks since the excitement at Morrison Middle School, and things there had started to return to normal. The science room had been mopped up and some new equipment installed. Of course, a science teacher was assigned, and it looked as if Charlie would be able to return to class before the end of the year.

I was back in the hospital. My little trip with Chockie had caused problems with my leg. Dr. Grinter was worried about it but not me. I knew now I'd be able to handle anything I had to.

The police decided that under the circumstances they wouldn't arrest Chockie for stealing the ambulance. The orderly who had his pants ripped off said his eye didn't really hurt that much and that he was proud his pants had helped solve the case.

I was resting in my bed when Charlie appeared in the doorway. He was in a wheelchair with one leg propped out in front and his right arm in a sling.

"Hi, William. I understand I missed some excitement at school."

"Hi, Charlie." I put my ragged copy of Denison on Detection down on the bedside table. "Come in."

His nurse carefully slid his chair between two flower displays, wheeled him up to my bed, and left us alone.

He smiled a wicked little smile. "I hear you turned on the Bunsen burner and blew old Dirk up."

"Yeah, but I almost blew my friend Andrea and me up, too."

He dropped his smile. "Oh, I'm sorry, I didn't hear about that. Is she alright?"

"Yeah, she ducked down behind the desk just before the blast. It was risky doing such a dangerous thing, but Dirk had a gun, and I was sure he'd have killed both of us."

"Sometimes we have to take chances."

Charlie shifted his weight in his wheelchair. I tried to get more comfortable too. The two of us squirmed around in our casts for a few seconds like we were doing some strange dance.

"I suppose they told you that you were right," he said. "Dirk is really Carl LePonte, Wraith's old accountant. The police caught Norma Owens too, and they told me that the two of them were indicted for conspiracy in attempting to murder me and on suspicion of murder in the death of the real Mr. Dirk, the guy LePonte was pretending to be.

"They also told me LePonte had been more or less living with Norma in the penthouse of your building since he disappeared from Wraith, so you had the case figured correctly. The only joker in the deck was his girlfriend, this Owens woman."

"And their only bad luck was that they lived in the same building with Chris, the trasher freak," I said. "But I guess they thought the old penthouse was a good hideout. It is close to the school so LePonte didn't have to go out in public often."

Charlie looked at me, then away, then back again. "I just wanted to say that when I lied to you about the police wanting your clues, well, I was wrong to do that. I was just so afraid that you kids couldn't handle the situation. I was afraid you might get hurt. Then it was my stupidity that caused all the trouble."

"You weren't stupid."

"Yes, I was. When I took a photocopy of the money band I left the extra copy in the machine. Then I fell for the oldest gag in the book and let Norma Owens lure me outside with a promise of *vital information*. I couldn't have made it easier for her to run me over if I'd tried."

"Even careful people have accidents," I said. "Just look at me."

He laughed then reached over and patted my hand. "Seriously, though, I'll never doubt your abilities again. You've as good a mind for detection as any I've ever encountered."

I looked past Charlie at a bunch of people who were coming through the door. Mom, Andrea, Chris, and Chockie. They fanned out around the bed and I introduced them to Charlie. He didn't say a thing, he just stared at Mom.

"You must excuse me," he said, "but you look so much like her, like—like someone I used to know."

"Goodness," she said. "That's the second time today someone said I reminded them of someone else."

"When was the first?" I asked.

"Just this morning your Ms. Vanderbur called about her nephew, Melrose. She said my voice sounded exactly like her astrologer's and she insisted I tell her what I saw in her stars."

Charlie was still staring at Mom. "Vanderbur? Katharine Vanderbur?"

"I believe she said, Mrs. Archibald Vanderbur."

"That's the one, Archie Vanderbur's widow," Charlie said. "She's a really famous lady, you know, one of the richest women in Chicago, probably the world."

"Really?" Mom said. "Well, *rich* Ms. Vanderbur said Melrose was back from the asthma clinic. She wants William to get started on her 'little problem' as soon as he gets out of here."

Charlie finally looked away from Mom and at me. "Vanderbur? William, you might wind up making more money than I do."

"Can I have a loan?" Andrea asked.

I winked at her. "I may get the money, but you get the fingerprint set."

"You can keep your fingerprint set, this time."

"But you found Chameleon."

"More like he found me," she said. "It was you who figured it out, I just accidentally found him. You're the greatest detective in the neighborhood."

"The greatest in the world," Chockie said, and he looked from face to face around the room. "Anybody got a problem with that?"

"Not me," Chris said.

Andrea slipped her hand in mine. "Me neither."

"No problem at all," Charlie said. "Absolutely the greatest in the world."

ORDER FORM:

NAME _____

ADDRESS _____

CITY _____ **STATE** ___ **ZIP** _____

NAME OF BOOK _____

QUANTITY _____

An invoice will be sent out with the books for payment...sorry we do not accept credit cards.

Discount 10% on orders over 10 copies.

Free shipping & handling on orders over 20 copies.

Press-Tige Publishing Company
291 Main Street
Catskill, NY 12414
(518) 943-0702 fax